THE

WEST LEIGH

MURDER

A Crime Story By

S R Lobban

This all stems from a dream, a bad one. One of those nightmares that is so visual, it was a relief to wake up. The memory stayed with me.

It has taken over 20 years to put pen to paper, or should I say finger to keyboard!

It is a work of fiction. Although the locations are real (and you can have a look on Streetview to check), all of the characters and events are either a product of the author's imagination or are used fictitiously. Any resemblance to actual persons, living or dead, or events is entirely coincidental.

He wasn't mad.

Of course he wasn't. Everybody has evil within them. Everybody. A sane man knows the difference between right and wrong. A madman doesn't. He knew what he was doing was wrong. So he wasn't mad.

The reason why he didn't feel that initial sense of revulsion was due to his strength of mind. He was strong enough to keep going. The sense of regret might come later. Maybe? But after the first puncture, he kept going. Due to strength, not madness.

And he planned everything. He knew what he was going to do and how he was going to do it. A madman wouldn't think that way.

No, he wasn't mad.

Monday 15th July 1996

The phone call came at 4.50am, only an hour before he was due to wake up. So he wasn't too bothered. He got out of bed, showered, dressed, went downstairs to his kitchen and ate some toast in his own time. 'They' weren't going anywhere. He even made his wife a cup of tea, which he took upstairs and put by the side of their bed. He kissed her good bye and then went back down the stairs and straight out of his front door.

It was hot, even at this early hour. This was going to be another scorcher, the sixth day of a heatwave apparently. He got into his Honda Civic and turned the key. As soon as the ignition came on, the radio started. He immediately turned it off. He loved music, not classical, but rock or pop or whatever was there at the time. He always had done. And to him, certain songs would take him back to a particular moment in his life. 'Anchors', they were known as. It was as if he had a soundtrack of his life. So, whenever he was going to see a body, he didn't want to have a song associated with it.

He drove off his drive and out of Princes, into Meadway and waited to turn left at the junction with Highfield Avenue. He saw the pile of newspapers that had been delivered to Devon's Newsagents. That's what he liked about this area. He knew that it would be an hour and a half before Nigel Devon would arrive to open up his shop. And he knew that all of those papers will still be there waiting for him. That wouldn't happen in other parts of Waterlooville. There were places where you couldn't leave anything out without it being screwed down.

He drove through into Ferndale and then on to the Hulbert Road. He only had three and a half miles to drive, so he could just take it easy. There was no traffic as he drove over the A3(M) and through the country road that took him in to Leigh Park. When he turned left in to Purbrook Way he started to let his mind think.

How old was he now? Forty-seven. That meant he had been with the Police Force for twenty-six years. Things had changed so much in that time. When he first started in 1970, a murder made headlines in the local papers and the story ran for days. Now there seemed to be a murder every week. "Messy murders" he called them. Fights that had gone too far or drug addicts taking it out on each other. But this one was going to be different.

He sat at the traffic lights at the junction with Petersfield Road, waiting for the green light. He knew that when he turned left he would see the murder scene. Less than half a mile away, straight ahead, there will be activity. He was two minutes away from a dead body.

He hesitated when the lights changed. For a split second, he considered turning right. Just to drive away, to give himself a bit more time. Go around the block, perhaps turn left in to Crossland Drive, go up New Lane, Prospect and come to the scene from a different direction. That would give him another five minutes or more before seeing the victim. It wasn't that he afraid of seeing a corpse, it was part of his job. He just hated seeing dead kids.

The thought passed, he released the handbrake and turned left. Up ahead, the road was closed. A dual carriageway with two squad cars parked across it. This will cause problems in an hour or two, he thought. A primary route into Havant and Portsmouth closed on a Monday morning, diversions through narrow, residential roads. The killer could have been a bit more considerate.

The road was closed just after the junction with Middle Park Way, so he pulled over and parked in the right-hand lane. Turned the engine off, took a breath, and opened his door.

The young constable didn't know who this tall guy was. He looked like a professor; Glasses, balding with a cropped beard and dressed in brown cords with a beige short sleeved shirt. His gangly frame ambled towards him.

"Morning, young man." He said. "You must be from Southsea."

"Yes" the young policeman replied, puzzled. And was about to start a well rehearsed speech to help protect the crime scene, when the professor walked straight past him. The words came out as a strange sound.

"It's alright mucker, I'll find my own way." And off he walked, towards Wakefords Way.

The crime scene was inside a copse, on the corner of the junction, opposite the walled garden of Staunton Park. Police tape had been wrapped around the trees and shrubs on the edge and a collection of vehicles were parked in the lay-by on the left-hand side of the road. Amongst them he noticed the Rover 620 of his Sergeant and a silver Toyota van. Two undertakers were standing beside it having a smoke, waiting to take the body to the mortuary at QA. Despite it being just before six in the morning, there were people standing in the gardens of their houses on the right-hand side. Word was going to get around quickly.

He knew the constable standing next to a gap in the trees, beside the lay-by.

"Hello Graham, you alright?"

"Morning Mister Finney, sir. Yes, I'm fine. Thank you for asking and you?"

"Well, I can think of better ways to come back from holiday. Lamden's in there I presume." Finney replied.

"Yes, sir. To be honest, I'm glad I'm out here. Not a nice one, sir."

"Hmm. It's a kid innit?"

"Yes, sir. Might be Teresa Gore."

This didn't mean much to Finney as his plane had landed at Gatwick six hours ago after two weeks of relaxing in a villa outside Cala Santanyi in Mallorca. He pulled a face and then ducked under the tape and followed a worn path through the copse. The scene of the action was less than fifty yards away. There was a circle of uniformed and plain clothed police. And in the centre, were a couple of men in white overalls crouched on their knees. A photographer, also in white overalls, moved in and around them. He saw the red hair of Sergeant Lamden.

"Ron!" he called

The red head looked up. "Oh, morning Guv. Welcome back. Did you miss us?" Lamden replied. A smile appeared, but it didn't last long.

"Yeah, I missed you like herpes. What's occurring?"

Lamden turned and walked around the outside of the group. Finney followed, looking at the Scenes of Crime Officers, while being filled in.

"A bloke walking his dog, came through here a few hours ago. His dog started digging and uncovered her. It's a girl. Under ten. In a bad state, multiple stab wounds. Oh, and the heat hasn't helped"

They stopped moving. From here, Finney had a clear view. He was at the feet of the girl. She had been buried, just. He could see the yellow material of her dress, just. There was brown hair, but little else to show where her head was. And there was a smell, a sickly-sweet smell that hung in the back of your throat. The SOCO team were taking samples and making notes. He wasn't sure if their masks kept the smell out. As he watched, he felt himself get drawn in. When Ron Lamden spoke, it snapped him out of it.

"We reckon it's Teresa Gore" Ron said. "An eight-year-old that went missing on Thursday night. There's been a bit of press about it in the rag, so uniform had the locals searching. As there haven't been any other girls disappearing, and she might have been wearing a yellow dress, it's probably her."

"Gore?" Finney asked.

"Yep. That's the one. Emily Gore's daughter. The poor cow had a shit life, and then ends up like this."

"Hmm. Did you say a bloke walking his dog? It's a bit early for that, innit?"

"Taxi driver. Works nights, comes home, walks his dog, goes go bed. I've got a feeling that he's not going to sleep for a while after this."

"Fair enough. Is Emily Gore still living in Forestside?"

"Yep"

"You hang on here 'til they've finished. Then we'll meet at the station." Finney said, not taking his eyes from the girl. "I'll go round and break the news."

He made his way back out of the copse. When he got to the tape, he looked up at the houses opposite. They were semi-detached and were at a higher level due to a grass bank next to the road. They had a grandstand view. There were now more people watching the activity, small groups talking to each other and nodding. To them, he was obviously a player. He ducked under the tape and walked to the left, he could see another marked car blocking Wakefords Way. He noticed that it had closed the road at the junction of Millbrook Drive. They would have to notify the Head of the school, next to the copse, that it will have to close for the day. That was someone else's problem. He turned around and walked back to the end of the road and crossed the deserted dual carriageway. As he got closer to his car, he saw a Volkswagen Transporter van parked on the left-hand side of the road. It had a dish on its roof and a small group of people gathered near the front. Press? He'd seen the live news channels but didn't think they would ever be in this neck of the woods. He went to the young constable.

"What's your name son?"

"Stafford. PC Stafford."

"Well I'm DI George Finney. You're doing a grand job so far, Stafford. Now you make sure that they stay over there. Right?"

"Er, yes sir."

Finney got into his car and started the engine. He was only going to be in the car for a couple of minutes, so switched the radio on. Terry Wogan spoke to him as he manoeuvred the car in a kind of U turn and then found a gap in the flow of traffic diverted from its planned route and drove south down Petersfield Road.

It took him four minutes. He turned left in to Bartons Road, then left in to Forestside Avenue with Wogan's patter and Johnny Cash singing 'Walk The Line' to keep him company. He parked outside the house, he didn't know the number but knew it was Emily Gore's.

He knew Leigh Park and West Leigh well. The first house he ever lived in was in Botley Drive. He only had vague memories of roads covered in clay and dirt as the estate was being built. Then he moved into Portsmouth at the age of four and stayed there until married life started. Then as a constable with CID based at Havant station, he really got to know the area.

Built after the Second World War to cope with Portsmouth's rising population, it was almost like an occupation. The city bought a huge area of land seven miles away from the city limits and built on it. The effect on the neighbouring town of Havant was to overwhelm it with council house residents and change the demographics forever. Then West Leigh was built, and roads such as this one were laid out on farmland. A few years ago, before a dawn raid on a serial burglar, George understood what the architects had in mind. In the early hours, the greens and buildings and garage areas made sense. They almost looked good. But architects never accounted for people. The problem with these areas was that when Portsmouth moved its residents, it also shifted its scum. He knew that less than ten per cent of the residents were bad, but this minority gave the area the worst of reputations. And being part of CID meant that he had got to know the area very very well.

He looked through the windscreen at Emily Gore's home. The end of terrace house still had the old windows and door, its paintwork peeling with age and neglect. He knew that the council were replacing these with double glazed units, but they clearly gave this one a miss. The glass on the door was reinforced with wire, but had been smashed, so a spider web of fractures covered it. He was first here three years ago, when another of her children had died. A six-month-old baby boy called Jason. Despite some initial concerns, it turned out to be a genuine cot death. No surprise considering the cocktail of drugs and alcohol that had been in its blood stream from the womb. He had made two more visits since then, both to deal with her partner's drugs dealing. The last time was eight months ago. George was happy with the four-year sentence that had been handed to Sam Tindall. Emily wasn't. But George hadn't been the only visitor from Hampshire Constabulary. Uniformed officers had called so often, to deal with noise, threats, domestic violence and general anti-social behaviour, that there wasn't a copper who hadn't heard of Emily Gore.

He got out of his car and tucked his wing mirror in, a habit in roads like these. There was no gate in the garden, which was overgrown and had the remains of a large motorbike leaning against front of the house. He could just make out the word Suzuki on the tank. It was probably nicked, he thought. At the door, he looked but there was no bell, so he rapped his knuckles on the window to the right of the door.

He wasn't expecting a quick answer, so was surprised when the door opened. A blonde boy, who George reckoned on being fourteen, peered around the edge. He was just about to speak when a voice bellowed from one of the back rooms.

"I told you, don't answer the farkin' door unless I tell you to!"

"I guess your mum's in then?" George said

The boy started to close the door, but George's foot pushed it back, causing it to spring open. At the end of the hallway, he could see Emily standing in the kitchen.

"Morning Emily" he said.

"What you doing 'ere Mister Finney, I've got enough on my plate as it is." She replied.

"It's about Teresa."

And with that, Emily turned and walked out of sight, the boy disappeared into the front room, on the left. George stepped into the hallway. He knew that these houses were maintained by the council and decorated every two years. It was obvious, that the decorators were due, because the place hadn't been cleaned since. The carpet was thick with grime, so thick that it had a gloss finish. The pale blue walls had dark greasy trails running along them. As he looked up the stairs on the right, he saw a girl dressed in dirty pyjamas. He knew this was one of the six-year-old twins. He made his way into the kitchen. Emily was leaning against the work surface, which was covered with dirty plates and pans. She took a cigarette, threw the packet on the side and turned a gas ring on and bent to light it.

To George, certain names created particular images. To him, Lucy was the name of a huge girl, who was so large she seemed inflated. Jayne was the name of a skinny, whiney girl. And Emily, well Emily was meant to be a pretty name for a pretty girl. But with Emily Gore, it just didn't fit. She was easily five foot eleven tall and weighed a good fifteen stone. A life of drinking and drugs had given her skin that matched George's beige shirt and had taken her teeth a long time ago. When she spoke, her voice was deep and there was a permanent slur. She took a drag off the cigarette and crossed her arms. George noticed that her T shirt and jeans were men's'.

"She's dead. Ain't she." She said, looking him straight in the eye.

The coldness in how she said it took his breath away, but then he realised it was obvious. He had been given the task of informing relatives countless times before. Most times it was obvious. They opened the front door, saw a copper and knew what that meant. Even in plain clothes, people knew.

"There's been a girl found in the woods, up the road. Might be Teresa. Was she wearing a yellow dress?" He asked.

"Could've been."

"Could've been? Don't you know?"

"I don't know what she was wearing. She goes out whenever she wants and does whatever she wants. She's eight years old, how am I supposed to know what she was wearing." Emily replied.

George looked at her in disgust, "She was eight years old, Emily. Was. What were you doing when you were eight years old? Eh? I know that you had a mum, and a dad, and a decent home. You had everything before you pissed it up the wall. Now tell me, what happened on the night that she disappeared." Not his usual way of breaking of bad news, he thought. But he knew he had hit her hard, because it was true.

Emily Gore was not a victim of society's problems. She grew up in a respectable part of Portsmouth. Her father worked in an executive role for St. Johns Ambulance, he was a spokesman and an ambassador for the charity. Her mother was Italian and stayed at home to raise her children, three of them. The only mistake these parents made was to send their children to the nearest school.

It wasn't a deprived, inner city hovel. It was in the centre of a middle-class Utopia. The problem was that most of the pupils came from the area, children of the town's tradesmen. Therefore, they didn't need an education, they were going to follow in their parents' footsteps. It wasn't cool to learn and as the kids had money, they could afford any of the drugs on the market. This is where all three of the Gore children went off the rails. Emily went the furthest.

She was sexually active at fourteen. Despite not being a looker, her large breasts and open legs made her popular with the male population of the north part of town. She conceived on her fifteenth birthday but didn't have a clue which one was the father. Her parents stood by her. But that wasn't good enough for Emily, so she left home and lived with a friend in a half-way house at Waterlooville. They would regularly sniff glue, smoke weed and whenever the opportunity came do crack.

The boy was born, and from then social support kicked in. She was given a flat in Paulsgrove, a prime location for illegal substances. That's where she met Sam Tindall, the father of the rest of her kids. When Teresa was born, she persuaded the Housing Office to give her a bigger home. That's when she moved to Forestside Avenue. Her parents still lived in the same house, but they'd never seen her since.

As George watched, her expression changed. She had lost the hardness in her stare. Her eyes glazed as she scanned the kitchen. She wasn't looking at the room, he thought, she's looking at her life. He wanted to lean, or relax, but didn't want to come in contact with any part of the room. When her eyes came to his, he saw the same look he had seen three years ago. Realisation. A registering of the fact that her lifestyle had destroyed one of her kids. Three years ago, he had hoped that losing a child would make her change her ways, but now he knew there was no chance of that.

He took a breath and said. "When did you see her last?"

"Thursday morning. That's when. Just before she went to school." There was a long pause. George could see her mind ticking over. "After that, I wasn't here."

"Booze? Or Crack?" George asked.

Emily looked to the floor and shook her head slowly. It was as if she was shaking the memory away. "Both."

George really needed to lean. He looked at the door frame at his shoulder height. It looked safe enough. He leaned his left shoulder against it and rubbed his beard with his right hand.

"She had a yellow dress, right?" He asked.

"I told the other coppers everything I knew when I reported her missing"

"But you haven't told me"

"She would always be out and about. Didn't matter what time of day or night. If she wanted, she'd walk round the estate. She had lots of friends, she'd see them whenever she wanted. And I didn't stop her, because I'm doing my own stuff."

She picked up the cigarette packet and lit another from the gas ring.

"On Thursday, I didn't miss her and Friday morning I assumed she had gone to school. It was about five on Friday that I first wondered where she was. I had a walk round and looked in different places. Obviously, I don't know who she mixes with, so I couldn't ask people. By nine, I was worried. I had no other choices, so I rung the police at ten. Don't look at me like that. I've already had you lot doing that and I feel like shit about it. Okay?"

George shrugged his shoulders. "What about the dress?"

"When they came round, we looked up in her bedroom. Her room is with the twins. They asked if any clothes were missing. The only one was her yellow dress, so I guess that is what she's wearing. Was wearing." Again, her eyes lost their focus.

"What about the boy? Did he see her?"

"Jack? He said that she was home on Thursday night. Had tea and that. She was wearing her school uniform when he saw her. And that is now on the bedroom floor, so she wasn't wearing that."

George looked out the open kitchen window into the garden. A large square of dry dirt with an old washing machine on its side. He remembered the brick shed at the end from his previous visit. He stood upright.

"Well. There will have to be a formal..." and then stopped. He was aware of someone coming down the stairs and it wasn't a child. He turned and looked through the doorway. A dark-haired man, dressed only in a pair of boxers, turned at the bottom. He looked into the front room, before walking towards George with his head down.

"Em?" he called. Then looked up and stopped abruptly. "Whoa."

George looked him up and down. About five feet, seven. Skinny, wiry build with a tattoo of a Chinese dragon across his chest. Scars on his arms. Dirty stubble on his chin. About twenty years old and he stunk. There was only one word for him, Scroat. On seeing him, the man turned and run back upstairs.

George turned back, "I guess he isn't a friend of Sam's. Emily? Like I was saying, there will have to be a formal identification. I'll let you know when."

He left her in the kitchen and walked to the front door. He opened it and paused. He looked to his right into the front room. The curtains were drawn and there was a glow from the television with a sound like MTV. The boy, Jack, was lying on a brown settee with his head on an arm. George could just see wet tracks on the boy's face reflecting the flickering light. Hmm, thought George, somebody's got a heart in this house.

George decided to drive back towards the scene before heading to Havant Station. He drove to the end of Forestside Avenue, turned left in to Oakshott and right in to Millbrook Drive. Immediately, he could see the effect of the road closure ahead. A flow of traffic was struggling to get through the narrow road and past the parked cars. When he got to the end of the road, after much stopping and starting, he looked left. The police car was still there across the road and a couple of hobby Bobbies were stopping parents and children going into the school. It might have been the heat, but by the look of it, they weren't coping with the stress very well. He noticed that the undertakers' van was still there. Perhaps the coroner wanted to see the girl in situ.

He turned right and then followed Wakefords Way to the end, where he turned right and left in to New Lane. Three minutes later he was driving into the quad at Havant Police station.

He had to choose where he was going to base his Incident Room. Although he had a choice of three stations nearby, this one, Waterlooville and Cosham, he decided to set it up at his own office, Fratton in Portsmouth. The stop off here was to gain some information about the 'Missing Persons' search for

Teresa Gore. After speaking with Sergeant Longe, he was up to speed.

The call had come in to Havant Station at nine fifty-three on Friday 12th July. There were reasons why there wasn't an immediate rush to respond. Because it was a Friday night, the majority of the uniformed officers were waiting to get their heads kicked in at Portsmouth's drinking hot spots. Guildhall Walk was such a volatile place that all the area's stations made up the thin blue line. Then there was the fact that it was Emily Gore making the report. She was one of the most disliked people in the Havant area, certainly by the police. So, it was a Panda car that happened to be in the area that called in at Forestside Avenue at ten, forty-two.

The two officers, one male, one female, took the details and a brief statement. They had reported that after looking through the wardrobe in the girls' bedroom that the lost girl was likely to be wearing a yellow dress. A radio message was sent out to any vehicles nearby to be on the lookout for Teresa.

The arrival of Saturday's day shift brought about the first searches. These were by beat officers checking out buildings, skips and various other hiding places. When a local resident informed the police that

Teresa was known for doing her own thing and going off for a while, the officers relaxed the intensity of their search.

Somehow the local paper, The News, had got wind of the disappearance and printed it as a front-page story in its Saturday edition. This forced the police to change gear. Again, because of hostility towards the Gore household, the community weren't interested, but Chief Inspector Harold McClintock didn't want Hampshire Constabulary to look bad in the public eye. So, he put on a display of uniforms, mainly local Special Constabulary volunteers, and organised a search on Sunday afternoon. With news crews from the regional television stations watching he had a line of constables swathing through the grounds and long grass of Staunton Country Park. It looked good on camera, but as the dog walker discovered on that morning, they were in the wrong place. Teresa was lying two hundred yards away to the east. And although he wasn't going to say out loud, George was quite pleased that the Chief was going to look like an arse.

After getting everything he needed, he drove out of the quad and on to Civic Centre Road. He wasn't sure, but he thought he had seen a guy with a camera on the grass outside. Was that the Press again?

His drive to Fratton station was easy. The traffic was flowing on the A27 and the M275 and he was turning in from Kingston Crescent waiting for the car park barrier to lift in under quarter of an hour. As he waited, he looked up at the grey concrete wall, with the sign 'POLICE Kingston Crescent'. If you were a civvy, a member of the public, this was Kingston Nick. But everyone in the force knew it was Fratton Nick. It hadn't been in Fratton for over thirty years, but the name stuck. And with it, came a sense of pride. Portsmouth coppers liked Fratton Nick. The barrier lifted and he slowly drove forward to his parking space. He got out of the car, nodded to a motorcycle officer and headed to the double doors in the shadows of the yard. He paused before opening the doors, enjoying the cool air, and then went inside, through the dingy corridor, caught the lift before the doors shut and pressed the button for the second floor. He stepped out of the lift, turned left and walked to his office, fourth door on the left.

It was stuffy in there and the air was stale. The first thing he did was go past the filing cabinets on the right and open the window. There was a desk against this window which had a kettle, mugs and a jar of coffee on it. He switched the kettle on, took the lid off the jar and poured some granules in to a mug and looked out the window while he waited. There was a building site opposite, a church for Mormons apparently. He thought whoever it was had plenty of money, by the standard of the work going on. The kettle boiled, he poured the water in to the mug and then took it with him as he sat down behind his desk. He straightened the photograph of his wife and two sons and then moved a small white pot with a blue design on it, it was a piece of Delftware. These were the two most important things in George Finney's life. He sat for a second, had a sip of coffee and considered turning his computer on. The thought of two weeks worth of e-mails put him off. Instead, he opened the drawer on the left of his desk, took out a blank sheet of A4 paper and a pen. Everything started with a blank sheet of paper.

The Incident Room had been set up in the conference room on the second floor, and the meeting had been arranged for three. George left his office at five to, walked right to the lift, then followed the corridor around to the left and continued to the door at the end. The conference room faced north, with no windows to the west or east, so it was cool. The day had proved to be another smouldering hot day, high eighties. Everyone George had met was wilting in the heat, but as he had only just come back from Mallorca, he was coping well.

He walked in. Opposite, all the windows were open and through these he could see the roofs of the terraced houses in the road behind. A long table was laid out from left to right, with chairs around. In these chairs, DS Ron Lamden sat on the far side next to Detective Constable Fiona Wells and Detective Constable Derek Marshall sat nearer the door. The length of the right-hand wall was covered with a pin board. SOCO photographs of the scene and Teresa were already pinned to the board. On the left-hand wall, Ordnance Survey maps had been pinned and covered with a large sheet of plastic, with hand written markers on it. There was a flipchart in front of this wall. As George looked around, he noticed that there were photographs on the same wall as the door. He recognised some of the faces.

"Afternoon everybody." He said. There was an assortment of replies. He sat down in the nearest chair. "Ron? D'you want to kick off?"

Ron Lamden stood up and moved to the left. He was wearing a pale blue shirt with his tie loosened and top button undone. His face had caught the sun and as he was fair skinned, he looked like he was blushing. He had his notebook, but he didn't refer to it as he started to speak.

"Right then. Welcome to West Leigh" as he waved his hand over the map, "A girl gets reported missing from her home in Forestside Avenue at ten o'clock on Friday night. Here. Monday morning, a girl's body is discovered in a shallow grave, here."

Both locations had been written with a dry marker.

"This copse where she was found, it's just a bit of woodland, that's leftover from the old estate. She was found here. The locals, school kids and that, use this bit as a shortcut. It's what people do, they always take the shortest route. So it's not a proper pathway, but it's become worn to a track. She was just two yards away from this track."

He paused in case anyone had a question.

There were none, so he continued, "First thoughts are that she wasn't killed here. There's not enough disturbance in the area to suggest that. This means she had to be carried to here. If you look at the map, you can see that the copse is a sort of square, but only two sides allow access. The South..."

Fiona Wells held a pen in the air.

"Yes Fi?"

"What about the other two sides?" She said.

Ron wasn't put off, "The North and East sides are only accessible through the school grounds. The gates were locked shut over the weekend, with the caretaker living in the lodge. We're talking about carrying a body without being discovered, so I believe we can rule out climbing over a six-foot-tall gate. The other two sides are next to the roads, Petersfield Road and Wakefords Way. As we saw this morning, the shortest distance is from Wakefords. It is likely that this would be the way the body would have been carried."

He paused again and saw that George was going to speak. This was an opportunity to open one of the bottles of water and pour himself a glass.

"I don't want to put a spanner in the works, Ron." George said. "But when I spoke to Emily Gore, she told me that Teresa was last seen on Thursday evening. That means the school grounds are an option. If the body was dropped off on Friday."

Ron pulled a pained expression, put his glass down on the table and looked back at the map.

George followed up, "But you're right about Wakefords being the easiest place to do it from."

"We'll have to make sure we question the caretaker." Ron said and nodded to Derek, who wrote some notes on a pad.

"The thing about this track is that everybody walks through it" Ron said. "And with the dry weather, there's no chance of footprints. One thing that SOCO said is that the killer will have burs on them. You know, from the vegetation in the copse. Trouble is, so will half the other people who have walked through there."

"Do we know about the time of death? Anything from the coroner's boys?" George asked.

"We had the main man himself, Mr Reginald Roadcliffe-Smith." Ron replied

"Yeah, well, there's Press involved already aren't there. McClintock wants to put on a show. So, time of death?" George repeated.

"No idea until after the Post Mortem, which will be tomorrow morning. The heat and the wildlife haven't helped us at all. There's a lot of decay"

"Hmm," George took his glasses off and rubbed his eyes and face. "Will there have to be a formal ID?"

"To be honest, they'll do it with dental records. Or an earring they found. But I think Gore deserves to see her daughter in that state. It might teach her a lesson."

George put his glasses back on and looked to Ron, who nodded to the woman.

"Okay Fiona, give me what you've got." he said.

Fiona Wells stood up and walked towards the photos on the pin board. She'd been in the force for ten years, two of those in CID. She wasn't butch, but it was clear she could handle herself. She wore a white blouse with a black skirt, she looked like she was in uniform. She got to the pictures of the scene and spoke slowly with a trace of a Yorkshire accent.

"Well, to carry on from Ron's words about the scene of discovery. It was a shallow grave, barely eight inches deep. The soil is very hard and clay like, so it would be a difficult task to dig up. And then she was covered over with the excavated soil, branches and ferns. It appears to be a quick job. It is apparent that the murder did not take place here, but there was a great deal of blood loss at this location. This would suggest that there was a very short period between killing and burial."

Fiona paused before moving to the photos of the victim.

"We are able to say that the victim was a girl wearing a yellow dress and that she had been stabbed repeatedly. Obviously, we'll have to wait for the results from the Post Mortem for accurate information. What can be seen from the photographs is that the weapon was a sharp instrument, but not a knife. This is an enlargement and you can see that one of the puncture wounds is almost rectangular. I think we're looking for a chisel or a screwdriver."

She stopped. The words hung in the air. It was as if all of them were visualising the last moments of Teresa Gore's life.

George cleared his throat and said. "Okay Fiona. Thank you. Derek?"

Fiona sat down as Derek stood up. He was the only one in the room wearing a jacket. He had a mop of brown hair with beads of sweat on his forehead. He looked like he was baking. He pointed generally to the photos on the wall. They were all mugshot combinations, front and sides.

"Twenty-three convicted kiddie fiddlers, nonces and paedos. All living within a half mile radius of the Gore house. We haven't got enough wall space for those living in the Leigh Park area."

Out of his team, George considered Derek the weak link. His work was like his dress sense... scruffy. He did have qualities, if you set him a task he'll do it but he couldn't think for himself. "And?" he asked, only just hiding his annoyance.

"Well. Ur, twenty-three possible suspects." Derek replied and with an afterthought, "Sir."

"Okay. Thank you, Derek."

Derek sat down as George continued from his chair, "I'm with you all on the theory of a quick job. I reckon you're right about there being little time between the killing and disposal. And I'm with you on the suggestion of the killer entering the copse from Wakefords."

He paused, looking at the map.

"If the killer needed to be quick, it was because there was a high risk of being discovered. This means if it was done in a house, someone else was in that house at the time. If it was outside, there was a chance of passers by. This may even suggest it was done in daylight."

He stood up and walked over to the pin board.

"Whoever did this was covered in blood. So they had to get cleaned up. Quickly."

He turned to his left and looked out the window at the roofs, his hands were in his pockets, his eyes taking in all the details. The three detectives sat and waited in silence. They noticed that the wall clock was ticking.

He turned to face the table. When he spoke, it was firm and decisive.

"We've got uniform doing house to house along that end of Wakefords Way and the roads off of it. Ron, I want you to see how they're getting on and find out about a bloke that's living with Emily Gore. Visit her if you need to. I found that he was scared of coppers, so it'll be worth finding out why. Fiona, Derek, I want you two to visit the members of your hall of shame here. But only the ones who are living with somebody. Wives, partners or lodgers. This wasn't done by someone living on their own. Alright?"

There was a chorus of "Yes sir."

"Any news, I'm on the mobile." George said and left the conference room.

He walked back to his office and sat down at his desk. With a sigh, he turned his computer on and got ready for the e-mail backlog to hit him.

George got home at seven that evening. Seeing the suitcase in the hall and the piles of washing in the conservatory reminded him that he had only been back at work for one day. The memory of sipping San Miguels by the pool of the restored finca seemed like months ago. Spending a day at Palma airport didn't help. A 'wildcat' strike by baggage handlers meant he and his wife had to endure an eighteen-hour delay. He was grateful they he had found somewhere comfortable to sit, the electric massage chairs. It was less than twenty-four hours since the taxi turned in to Princes Drive, with both of them fearing a burnt-out shell of a house to welcome them back. Then their concern was whether their sons had trashed the house. All was fine. No fires and no trashing.

To be fair, their boys were old enough to be trusted. The oldest, Neil, worked in a mobile phone shop. So much for getting a degree in Business Studies, George thought. And the youngest, Ian, was happy as an apprentice plumber. His boss was a good friend of the family. They were both good lads. At twenty-two and nineteen, George wondered when he would stop thinking of them as lads.

During dinner, his wife, Cheryl, had said that George was seen in the regional news coverage of the murder. It must have been when he was walking back to his car. Apparently, it was a short piece, with a sound bite provided by Chief Inspector McClintock. After the meal, Cheryl settled to watch telly and George retired to the front room. This was his space.

There was a dining table in the middle, made from dark wood, and four matching chairs. It was only used at special occasions like Christmas. The rest of the time it was strewn with paperwork, sewing boxes and random household items. If something got lost, this was the place to start looking. Today, it had a pile of post. Two weeks worth of junk mail, utility bills and a few, just a few pieces of decent correspondence. There was also the day's edition of The News and a parcel, about the size of a shoe box. George sat down at the table, looked at the display cabinets on either side of the chimney breast, and the photos on the wall opposite and then got stuck in to the pile.

As he started, he thought about the rest of his day. The e-mails were easy to get through with nothing important, just internal messages. There hadn't been any real progress in the Gore case, though. They were waiting on the Post Mortem. Door to door enquiries had drawn a blank and were being extended to take in the whole area from Bartons Road in the south to Wakefords Way in the north and Petersfield Road to the west and Prospect Lane in the east. This was likely to be the only area Teresa Gore moved around in. Somebody must have seen her. They hoped. McClintock had ensured all available uniform officers were being used. Another display for the media, George thought.

No weapon had been found, but this was to be expected. The discovery scene wasn't where the crime took place.

DS Lamden had taken the earring, which had been found on the body, to Emily Gore for identification purposes. It was Teresa's. Ron had also said that he got a name for the scroat, Steven Armitage. He was one of West Leigh's finest. As a juvenile, he had a long list of breaking and entering and motor theft. Two years ago, on his eighteenth birthday, he was caught whilst trying to break into the Co-op shop at the far end of Forestside Avenue. He was given a six-month sentence but was out in three. In those three months, he had honed his skills and while being suspected of many things, had managed to avoid any more charges.

Of Derek Marshall's twenty-three possibles, only seven were living with other people. He and DC Wells had visited them all. Two of them were still on the list. Depending on the results of the Post Mortem, they could be pulled in for questioning. Not wanting to take any risks, George asked for both of them to be watched. Both constables were single, so they were happy to get paid for sitting in a car overnight.

George had dealt with all the mail except for the parcel and had a large pile for the bin and a small pile to be filed in the drawer of the dresser, beneath the photographs. Before opening the package, he looked at the newspaper. The headline read "Body Found in Woods" with a sub heading of "Police searching for missing girl make a grisly discovery". There was a photograph of McClintock accompanying the story. He had also provided a quote, "Every measure will be taken to catch the monster responsible for this." Typical, thought George. He had no time for McClintock. It wasn't that he had been in the force for a shorter time, it wasn't that he was younger. George didn't mind ambition, but he liked workers, grafters, not climbers.

He had joined the Hampshire Constabulary two days after his twenty first birthday, trained at Netley, then started off as a PC on the beat in Portsea. He settled in, made his mark in one of the roughest areas of town and was happy. His first inkling to try for promotion was when he planned to marry Cheryl.

And he got it and off he went to Waterlooville station. He expected an easier time, it was almost rural, or so he thought. But there were two areas being developed nearby to take more of the overspill from Portsmouth. And of course, Portsmouth weren't getting rid of their decent citizens. George found himself dealing with Wecock Farm, and Mill Road. It took a little while and he took some knocks, but he made his mark again.

He became involved in the investigation of a boy's murder in 1983. The fourteen-year-old, Timmy Young, was known to George as a petty thief. Because of this, he looked in to his last movements and passed on the information to CID. It turned out the lad had broken into the home of Eric Baker, the Grandfather in one of the nastiest families on the estate. Two days later, Reginald and Frank Baker met Timmy on a walkway across Eagle Avenue and kicked him to death. The Detective Inspector in charge recommended that George should join CID. George followed up the recommendation two years later, after refusing an offer for promotion to be a uniformed Inspector. He had always viewed uniformed senior officers as vain trophy hunters. McClintock was one of the worst. He had come out of university and got himself fast tracked, gaining promotion at the earliest opportunity. George felt he had very little real policing experience and couldn't keep out of the media spotlight. This case was proving to be another example of that. He didn't bother reading anymore of the report, he knew there was nothing of substance, so he threw the paper on the bin pile and turned his attention to the package.

If you were watching closely, you might have sensed there was a smile on his face as he carefully undid the tape and opened the brown box. Inside there was a bundle of bubble wrap. He slowly turned the box so the bundle fell gently in to his right hand. Then he unravelled the wrapping and bit by bit revealed a Toby jug, just over six inches high and weighing less than two pounds. It was white porcelain with blue detail, an example of nineteenth century Dutch Delftware. He had ordered it before going on holiday and although he wouldn't have admitted it to Cheryl, he was thinking about it while he was out there. It was going to be another piece to go on display in the cabinets to his right, making fifty-two items. The first piece of Delft he ever had was a plate, given to him by his Grandfather who had received it as a wedding gift. George was seven years old and he loved the fine detail in his favourite colour, blue. As he grew older he bought a few more pieces and began to appreciate their age, and whether it was the future detective in him, he would imagine who owned them or what events they had survived. He didn't broadcast the fact he collected these bits of pottery, but word had got out. As a new member of CID, he got ridiculed by the other detectives. He had heard some of the nicknames, Professor, Dullard, Mr Grey and much worse. They still continued behind his back, but he didn't care. He never did. He was happy with the image he projected. He wouldn't let anyone know that he'd spent the last two weeks water skiing and scuba diving. He wanted them to think he was boring.

Just before he joined the force, he heard a phrase used by American Hot Rod kids of the sixties. It was used to describe a car that looked like nothing, but had been tuned to perfection and, as George would say, "Go like shit off a shovel!" Everybody underestimated it, never thought it was a threat and would lose. George wanted people to underestimate him. George Finney wanted to be a 'Sleeper'.

Tuesday 16th July 1996

George drove into the entrance of Queen Alexandra Hospital at five to eight the next morning. He was happy to have the radio on, so Wogan had kept him company along London Road. He parked in one of the reserved spaces next to the mortuary building. Ron Lamden was standing by the door smoking, he took a last drag and dropped it on the ground.

"Morning Guv"

George noticed that Ron was redder than yesterday and had sweat patches on his pale green shirt. "Blimey Ron, you've had quite a workout with that fag."

Ron looked down at his shirt. "Eh? Oh, no. I parked my car in Cosham Nick and walked up here. This heat is going to do me in. Roadcliffe-Smith's in there already."

He pointed to the single storey building with his thumb.

"Come on then." George said and the both went in.

They spent two and a half hours in the cool, disinfected air of the mortuary. When they stepped outside, the heat hit them hard. The written Post

Mortem report was going to be sent later, but they had enough information to work with. George took out his mobile phone and after dialling, issued his instructions to the voice on the other end. He took Ron back to Cosham to pick up his car, and then drove down London Road and Northern Parade to head back to Fratton station.

The Incident Room had become a hive of activity. More photographs were on the right-hand wall, and more writing was on the map. Detective Constables Webb and Marshall sat at different ends of the table with coffee cups, Pro-plus and statements in front of them. They looked shattered. There were also three uniformed officers, one working with a computer and the other two working through paperwork. George walked in and went to the flipchart, he turned the sheets until he found a clear page. When Ron Lamden came in and sat down, George looked around the room.

"Okay ladies and gentlemen, if I can have your attention please." Everyone in the room looked his way. As he spoke he wrote key words on the paper.

"We have information from the Post Mortem and I'm going to get you all up to date. We are dealing with the murder of Teresa Gore. There was a positive identification from some medical history, there will also be a check with dental records. Unfortunately, we haven't had a great deal of luck with the time of death. The PM shows that a meal was eaten around Thursday evening, but that's it. The heat has accelerated the decomposition so that's the best we can get. She was stabbed a total of forty-three times with a sharp instrument."

Something had caught his eye. McClintock had entered the room and was standing near the photographs.

"As you mentioned yesterday Fiona, it was a weapon with a rectangular cross section that measured four millimetres by fifteen. Most likely a chisel, but he wouldn't say for definite. The angle of the entry wounds suggests it came from the victim's right-hand side, with most of the wounds in the chest and abdomen. Nothing to the face. The fatal wounds were two to her right lung, along with the blood loss, she would have passed out and then drowned when her lung filled up. She was not sexually assaulted."

He looked at the officers and could see a look of surprise.

"On this occasion. But there has been sexual activity in the past."

Lamden and Marshall both let out a noise, it could have been the word "Shit".

George continued, "There didn't appear to be evidence of a struggle. Nothing under her nails, to suggest she fought back and scratched her attacker. There were no traces of anyone's tissue were found at all. But..."

He wanted to ensure he had their attention. All eyes were on him.

"Her clothes and hair had traces of urine on them."

Derek Marshall couldn't stop himself, "He pissed on her! What kind of sick bastard does all that and then pisses on her. If I get my fu..."

He was cut short by George, aware of McClintock's gaze.

"You'll wait at the back of the queue. We're all going to feel het up about this piece of shit. But we're going to deal with him properly. And what has happened, by this discovery is that he has given us a massive helping hand in finding him. There is a new thing come about called DNA. If they can get a trace of it from his piss, we can pin our man as soon as we've got him. But we have to get him first. Okay?"

Marshall sheepishly agreed.

George had stopped talking and looked at the points he had written on the flipchart.

He read, "Thursday evening. 43 times. Chisel? No face. Not sexual. Historic. No defence. No tissue. Urine."

He looked at the far end of the table. "So? Fiona?"

Fiona Wells had studied Psychology at Leeds University before joining the police and while she wasn't fully fledged, he liked to hear how she viewed things.

She looked at the board for a minute before speaking.

"My first thought is that we are dealing with someone who knew her. If you are going to stab someone forty-three times, you are either a savage lunatic or emotionally involved. The likelihood of having a mad axe man wandering the streets is so unlikely it has to be an emotional attack. Also, if you consider that there were no defence wounds or indication of a struggle, she had to be led in to a position mutually before being attacked. Therefore, she knew who he was. I would say that this theory is backed up by the lack of wounds to her face. Her killer couldn't bring himself to damage it. Perhaps this would tarnish his memory of her. I wouldn't be surprised if he covered her head, so he didn't have to look at her."

All the time she was speaking, she had been looking at the words. When she stopped, she looked at the others in the room. They were all nodding.

"What about the urine?" George asked.

"I've heard that some killers have masturbated over their victim. It's like the act of killing has turned them on so much that they have to ejaculate. Perhaps in this case he couldn't get it up, so he weed on her?" She replied.

"Might be the final insult?" It was Ron, he continued, "You know, I'll piss on your grave."

"Could be." Fiona said. "This again leads to a personal reason for the killing. A stranger wouldn't warrant this kind of insult."

The room went quiet. Each person thinking about this suggestion. George paced from the flipchart to the wall on his right. There were three mugshot photographs alongside the door, two were remaining from the previous day, the other was an addition, Steven Armitage.

He looked at the faces as he spoke. "When I got the information at the Post Mortem, a couple of things struck me. Of your two remaining sex offenders, Derek, one of them, Robert Johnson, had a regular method of operation. He always threatened his victims with a screwdriver. Did you know that?"

"No sir." Marshall replied.

"Hmm. So, he was one of the people I wanted to speak to. The other is Armitage, here. If there's a recent history of sexual abuse. It has to be at home and it's got to be him."

He tapped the photo.

"If you take in to account what Fiona has just said, he becomes an even bigger suspect. Would you all agree?"

There were nods of approval from everyone including McClintock. George turned to him.

"Did you arrange for them to be picked up and brought here?"

"I issued the instructions just after you called me, George. They should be downstairs shortly."

"Alright then. Thank you" George said and added in a quieter tone, "Sir."

"All sounds as if it's in hand. You'll keep me informed. Won't you?" McClintock said and left the Incident Room.

"Oh yes sir and I'm sure you'll notify the press" George whispered.

George was right.

As soon as McClintock put the phone down on his request for two suspects to be brought in, the Chief Inspector called his contact at The News and his new acquaintance from BBC News.

He had been waiting for this moment a long, long time. He had watched rolling news emerge from the birth of digital television. He knew that if he was given the opportunity, he could shine in this new style of reporting. It would help him in his climb to the top. He had seen other police chiefs around the country when a major incident had occurred. And he was jealous. He knew he would look good in front of the cameras, he would be known nationwide, all he needed was the right crime. And this was perfect. Everyone wanted to know about a murdered child and the hunt for its killer. This was it. If he was honest, he would have preferred a more respectable mother. It would have looked better if he could have been filmed with the grieving parents alongside. There was going to be little sympathy for a drug addict. So it was best to brush over her and concentrate on him and the hunt. The footage had looked good so far. The sweeping shots of uniformed policemen searching for the missing girl were very pleasing to the eye. He'd got off the hook about looking in the wrong place by saying that the woods were going to be searched the following day, and the dog walker beat them to it. Anyway, police searching woodland wouldn't have looked as attractive. He had been happy with his sound bite on the previous day, although a little disappointed that it only featured in the regional report. But today was going to be different. Today would have plenty of door to door footage and there was going to be national interest.

With this in mind he had instructed two squad cars, each with three officers to go to the two suspects' houses. He ordered them to collect the suspects and to not arrive at Kingston Crescent until he gave the word. He made sure that there would be cameras waiting for them as they drove into the station. He would then be available for comment.

 The two cars left Havant station at the same time. Both drove to Petersfield Road and headed north until they reached Bartons Road. They both turned right at the traffic lights, one turned left in to Forestside Avenue and stopped at Emily Gore's, the other turned left in to Prospect Lane and pulled over on the right-hand side, stopping half on the pavement. All the officers got out and made their way into Gosport House. They went in the first door, climbed the concrete steps to the next floor and stopped at the second door. The driver knocked on the reinforced glass with his knuckles. A woman in her fifties came to the door, she looked through the stippled glass and then opened it a little. She was half asleep. Even if she was fully awake she wouldn't have been prepared for what happened next. The three officers pushed their way in, shouting "Police" and giving details of why they were there. They headed straight for the bedroom door behind her to the right and pulled the sleeping lump from the bed. Robert Johnson was pulled up to his feet and as he was wearing pyjamas, marched out of the room and out of the flat. The woman was screaming behind them, causing neighbours to open their doors and have a look. The commotion was enough to disturb the next block up, so these residents looked out of their bedroom windows to see him being dragged, shoeless, into the squad car. The whole operation took less than five minutes.

The officers at Forestside Avenue didn't have it as easy. After stopping, getting out and banging on the door, they didn't get an answer. The boy, Jack, just peered down on them from his bedroom window and the twins watched from the top of the stairs. Emily and Steven Armitage were asleep in the back bedroom and only a bomb would wake them. Or a front door being kicked in by three policemen. The door gave way with a loud crack which went through the house. The shouting began and Armitage woke up before they had started up the stairs. As they came running he opened the window and climbed through. It was an eleven foot drop, so he got himself in to a position to hang and dropped to the garden. When they kicked back the bedroom door, Emily Gore started screaming. They were shouting back when one saw Armitage, dressed in his pants, climbing over the brick wall into the back yard of the flats. The policemen ran back down the stairs and out of the house. They ran across the front garden, jumped over the low wall and headed round in to the flats' entrance in Curdridge Close. They couldn't get in. The doors needed a security code. An officer pressed different numbers until someone answered. One of the officers was thinking and realised that if they couldn't get in, nor could Armitage. He jogged back to Forestside Avenue and looked down the road just in time to see a man dressed only in his pants running across the grass, heading towards Whitsbury Road. He shouted back and started running. The other two followed. The driver got back into the car, leaving the one to follow his colleague.

They finally caught Armitage in Oakshott Drive. He had run though the alleyway from Whitsbury and was only worrying about the two policemen behind him. So when he ran out of the alley, he hadn't anticipated that the driver of the squad car was going to be there to rugby tackle him. When the other two got there, all three made sure that he had some bruises before putting him in the back of the car.

Both cars radioed back and co-ordinated their arrival time with McClintock. And, exactly as planned, the cameras were there for their arrival.

When George received the call that the two suspects had arrived, he and Lamden made their way down to the Interview Rooms. Of the two, he thought Johnson was the least likely, but because of his history he had to speak to him. He decided that he would be the first they spoke to.

When the two detectives opened the door to Interview Room 2, Robert Johnson was sitting at a table in the middle of the room. The door opening and their footsteps on the tiled floor stirred him as if he had woken up. Still in his pyjamas, he had smoothed his hair down and arranged it to a side parting, his eyes were red and he looked older than his sixty-four years. He watched them as George and Ron took the two seats opposite. Ron put down a pad and removed a pen from his shirt pocket, George put down his cup of coffee.

"Mornin'" he said. "I'm Detective Inspector Finney, this is my colleague, Detective Sergeant Lamden. You comfy?"

Johnson just looked at them with his arms folded tightly across his chest.

"Cup of coffee?" George asked.

Johnson remained still. He looked at the detectives one at a time, then looked down at the table, sighed and shook his head.

"When are you going to let me forget?" He said. His voice was very articulate and educated. Ron looked up from his notes in surprise, but not George.

"I mean. When are going to allow a man to get over his mistake?" Johnson continued.

"Mistake?" George asked.

"It's been ten years"

"Yeah and you were inside for six of those."

"Exactly. Six years. I was cut, beaten, sodomised, don't you think I've paid my price for a slip." He unfolded his arms and put his hands on his lap.

"A slip? Is that what you call sexually abusing ten-year-old school kids. And raping little girls while holding a screwdriver to their neck."

"Once."

George leaned forward. "You were caught once. And charged once. And sentenced once. But there were six attacks, which stopped when you were locked up. Funny that. And then you got out of prison, come down here and got yourself a nice little flat, a hundred yards from a school"

He sat back in his chair, picked up his cup and sipped while watching Johnson.

"Your friend? Back home. Does she know what you've got up to?"

"Caroline is a very understanding lady." Johnson replied.

"You see the thing is Robert. Ladies don't like kiddie fiddlers. So I reckon that she's involved with you. Is that how it works? The two of you, coaxing kids into your pokey little flat."

Johnson looked George in the eyes and when he spoke it was a resigned, tired whisper.

"Why don't you get to the point? I know what this is about. The Gore girl. I've seen it in the papers. I thought you'd come knocking when she went missing."

"When my colleagues called last night, they asked you a question. Where were you on Thursday evening?" George asked.

"I stayed in. On my own."

"Where was your friend, Caroline?"

"She was at work. She works at a nursing home near Rowlands Castle as a carer."

"And when did she come home?"

"She finished at twelve."

"So nobody can back you up, being in all night. Alone. And of course, Caroline will confirm that you're a good boy now."

Johnson dropped his head in to his hands.

George looked and then sucked air through his teeth and made a sort of tune.

"We're going to search your flat."

Johnson looked up, his voice was dry. "Look. I know what you think I am. I know what I am. Six years in prison made me realise what I did was wrong. I think I have a disease. You think I'm a sick twisted bastard. But if you knew how hard it is for me. To stop myself. To resist the temptation. It's been so difficult at times I've thought I should end it all."

"My heart bleeds."

"Search my flat. There's nothing to find. I didn't do anything. She hasn't been there. I have never seen her. Do what you like, because after this morning, my life is fucked."

"Alright Robert. We'll do that."

George leaned forward, he was inches away from Johnson's face.

"But if we find so much as a sweetie wrapper, I'll come down on you like a ton of bricks."

George moved his chair back, looked to Ron, stood up and made his way to the door. Ron picked his pad and pen up and followed leaving Johnson staring in to space.

George seemed to remember something when he got to the door.

"Oh yes. Robert? If you ever have that feeling again. You know, that you want to end it all. Give me a call."

Johnson's eyes focused on him, his face had a curious look.

"Yeah, 'cause I've got plenty of rope." George opened the door and left.

Outside they walked along the corridor to a phone on the wall outside Interview Room 3. George picked it up and dialled the extension for the Incident Room. He waited a second.

"Can I speak to DC Marshall, please." Another second or two. "Derek? Arrange a search warrant for Robert Johnson's flat. Take someone from Forensics to look for any evidence, hair, blood, anything to do with kids, you know the score. And ask Fiona to check the latest from the woods. See if anything new has come up. Thanks."

When he put the phone down, he looked at Ron. He could tell he needed a smoke.

"Come on, have a quick fag. Then we'll go and see Armitage."

"Cheers Guv. What do you think about Johnson?" Ron said feeling his pockets for the packet and lighter.

They walked along the corridor to a Fire Exit. George opened the door and they stepped out into the car park before he spoke. They were in shadows but it was still hot.

"He's not our killer. It's not his style. He's been up to something though."

"I didn't expect the accent." Ron said, lighting up.

"He was a head teacher up near Oxford. Used to get the kids to do sexual favours for him and then threaten them so they kept quiet. Private school and all that."

"Bastard"

"Hmm, he didn't get sent down for that though. No. He only got a suspended sentence for it and then moved to a different town and starting raping kids."

They stood in silence while Ron sucked on his cigarette. When he finished, he threw the butt down.

"Ready Guv" He said.

"Good. You take the lead on this one to start off with, okay? I want to sit and watch the little turd for a while."

When they walked into Interview Room 3, they were hit by the smell of stale body odour. Steven Armitage was wearing white paper overalls, but still had nothing on his feet. As he turned to the door, they could see scratches on his face and swelling over his left eye. It was almost like deja vu for the detectives. Same pale green walls, same tiled floor, same table and chairs in the middle and their suspect sat at the table, arms folded across his chest. They took the same seats opposite.

As Ron went through the introductions, George watched them both. For a second, he thought of it as being a fly on the wall's view. Which going by the smell wouldn't have too far fetched. He heard Armitage grunt as he slid his chair back, got up and walked over to a small dial on the wall. As he turned it there was a click and the sound of air being blown in. He sat back down and hoped the smell would disperse quickly.

"What d'you want a solicitor for?" he heard Ron say. "We're only 'aving a chat."

He liked Ron Lamden. A lot. He was a grafter like George and should work his way to the top. He'd have to do it quick though, before the new breed came in. The university boffins who knew nothing of the real world. So far CID didn't have many people like McClintock, but it wouldn't be long. Ron had grown up in Selsey, just outside Chichester. It surprised George how rough he was, as he always thought it was a posh place. But it did mean he would get to the bottom of things and didn't mind ruffling feathers.

"The uniformed officers came round on Friday night, when Teresa was reported missing, but they didn't get a statement from you. How come?" Ron asked.

"I was out." Armitage replied.

As George looked at him, he considered how attitude changes appearance. Armitage was resting back in the chair with his legs straight in front, like he was a board leaning against the chair. With his arms folded and chin on his chest, he was staring at Ron under dark eyebrows. It made him look fairly intimidating. Hard. But as George watched him give arrogant replies, he could see that he was basically a wimp. George thought of his own boys, one older by a couple of years and the other younger by a year. They were both better looking than Armitage, they were also better built than Armitage, but if you'd put them side by side, you would fear Armitage and dismiss his boys. The thing was, everything Armitage had was a show. It would be easy to break him down and get to the real boy underneath.

"So." Ron said. "Tell me about Thursday evening. Everything. Tell me about the last time you saw Teresa."

Armitage blew out some air and then said. "Suppose the last I saw 'er was Wednesday, yeah, Wednesday night."

"Not Thursday?"

"Nah. Was busy Thursday. Didn't see 'er then at all."

Ron spoke in a low voice, with just a hint of menace. "Busy? Where? Bedroom? Front room? Garden? It's a murder investigation. I want to know what you were doing."

"'S with Emily, weren't I. 'S doin' stuff an that."

"Just tell me what the fuck you were doing Thursday!" Ron shouted. It made Armitage flinch.

"Look. We had some gear and some cans from the Co-op and got wasted. Alright? We was totally out of it. In 'er room. Bedroom. Didn't come out until Friday. Don't know what time it was. I know that it was about five o'clock when Em starts saying about the kid. She starts 'aving a right ol' go about 'er. Where the fuck is she an' all that. Starts 'aving a go at me, saying it's my fault, but I ain't 'ad nothin' to do with it. So I says she'll turn up. Don't worry an' that. But it gets later and later. Well, at nine she says she's gonna call the old bill. I said to her, I said don't be fuckin' stupid. We don't want the filth round 'ere. She said she 'ad to do soming, so I says well open the windows and leave it for a bit before you ring up. That was it. When she rung up, I went out. Didn't wanna 'ang about with you lot around. So I went over near The Fox. Well out the way."

Ron leaned back and looked at George. He gave a nod.

"Steven. Is it Steven? Or is it Steve? I guess it would be Steve. Because it's not that cool to be known as Steven is it?" George said with an emphasis on the 'en'.

"No. It must be Steve. Fits the image doesn't it? Rock hard Steve. Yeah, 'cause you're really quite a legend, aren't you? Steve. Car thief Steve. Burglar Steve. Drug dealer Steve. Yeah, it does fit. Whereas Steven would be the name of a nonce. Wouldn't it? Steven the paedophile. That sort of goes doesn't it."

He looked at Armitage, the image was beginning to crack. Then gave a Ron a quick glance, so he would know what was coming next. When he next spoke, it was as if he was pondering, his hand come to his mouth in thought.

"So, how old are you now, Steve?"

"Twenty"

"Twenty? Umm. When're you twenty-one?"

"September."

"September! So you're nearly twenty-one. Cuh, twenty-one, eh? Blimey. Still, you've done well for yourself, haven't you? I mean you've got..."

He stopped, thought for a bit, then continued. "Oh no, you haven't, have you? You're shacked up with some other bloke's bird."

Armitage changed position in his chair, his legs crossed and moved so they were underneath it. He tried to keep his upper half in the same position, so he could keep an aggressive front.

George took his glasses off and rested them on the table. The change of appearance made a change in attitude. With his glasses on, he knew he looked safe, soft and perhaps bumbling. But without his glasses, he looked hard, tough and unbreakable. He carried on.

"You know Sam, don't you Steve? You know, Sam? Sam Tindall? Big Sam? Ooh he is big, really big. Isn't he Ron?"

Ron silently nodded back.

"Yeah, big Sam. Oh yeah and when he gets angry."

He puffed out some air and shook his head.

"How many of us did it take to pin him down, Ron? When we nicked him. Four? Five?"

"At least" said Ron. He was enjoying watching George at work.

"Well, I wouldn't want to upset big Sam Tindall. No way. Hmm"

There was more shuffling from Armitage. He was now sitting upright.

George kept going, "I think, I'm not sure, but I think Teresa was one of Sam's. Let me think now. The boy wasn't, no. But Teresa and the twins, yep, they're Sam's. Funny that isn't it, Teresa being Sam's girl. Hmm. Yeah."

He paused to allow it to sink in, gazing just above Armitage's head and then gave a snigger.

"That would be funny, wouldn't it Ron? If Steve here and Sam were in the same prison. Eh? Wouldn't that be something. Maybe even in the same cell."

Armitage sprang forward, his hands on the table, leaning in to the two detectives and screamed "You can't do that! You're bluffin', you wouldn't be able to, I got rights, you..."

"Sit down and shut up!" George shouted back.

Armitage threw himself back in to the chair. His eyes were red, he was sweating and breathing heavily. The armoured shell had been broken. He looked like a skinny runt.

"So how long have you lived with Emily Gore?" George barked

"Since January." Armitage answered quietly. He had lost his attitude.

"A month after Sam Tindall was banged up. That's nice. What did you do, sniff around and find out that she was on her own?"

"I used to get gear off of Sam. I went round there and 'e wasn't there. She told me what 'ad 'appened. I just stayed. Been there since."

"But what's the appeal about Emily Gore? I mean she's a moose."

"She's alright" Armitage was now staring at the table.

"Alright? Not being funny, but I'd go gay instead of getting hooked up with that. I've heard of any port in a storm, but there are limits."

Armitage said nothing, but Ron had to stop himself from sniggering.

"I know what the appeal was." George said.

He waited in silence until Armitage looked at him. He stared him in the eyes and then said.

"Eight-year-old Teresa Gore. That was the appeal. It was worth putting up with the beast, because you had access to what you wanted. Sex with an eight-year-old girl. What was it? Was she irresistible to your charms or did you force yourself on her every time? Because it was more than once, wasn't it? You kept on forcing yourself on her and making her keep it a secret. And then one day she said she was going to tell. She was going to make sure everyone knew the truth about the local legend Steve. And you couldn't have that, could you? So you took a chisel from the shed and you took her to your dirty, little, secret place and stabbed her. Not once, not twice, but over and over and over until you knew she was dead."

Armitage screamed, "I didn't kill her! I didn't. I lu..."

George stopped him with a slow, stone cold voice. "If you dare say that you loved her, I'll punch you so hard."

Armitage shrunk in his chair and sobbed, his shoulders moving up and down. When he spoke bubbles of spit came from his mouth. "I didn't hurt her. I never could have hurt her. I was always gentle with her."

George looked at Ron and gave a nod. With that Ron began to caution Armitage. As he was speaking George looked up to the right-hand corner of the ceiling, he picked up his glasses and put them on to see that the light on the video camera was on. That might come in handy later, he thought.

George left Ron to deal with Armitage and his statement. After leaving the Interview Room, he checked that everything they had done had been filmed. It was clear that they had been given some form of a confession. Enough to charge the man.

He went straight to his office and contacted his team. Derek Marshall was still inside Johnson's flat with a couple of Forensics officers having a good look round. They had found a stash of fetish gear, but nothing connecting him with Teresa Gore. One thing that might have been of interest was his computer, so they were going to bring that back to be checked out. Fiona Wells said that the SOCO team in the copse were struggling because the pathway had been used by so many people. They had taken soil samples to check for traces of urine. She had spoken to the caretaker of the school, but nothing suspicious had been seen. He asked her to take the team to the Gore house and look for a possible weapon and any traces of blood. The last thing he did was contact McClintock to get him up to date. The Chief Inspector asked to see George at four o'clock.

After putting the phone down, he looked at the piece of paper on his desk. It was laid in a landscape form. He had written 'Teresa' in the centre, at the top. 'Thursday evening' was written on the left-hand side and Monday on the far right. He wrote 'Armitage' under 'Teresa'. He sat looking at the paper, his pen tapping gently on the desk. Something was troubling him.

He spoke quietly. "Monday? No. Sunday? No. Saturday? No. Friday? Friday, could be. Thursday, could be."

He then wrote 'Time?' and circled it.

"Why did nobody see her?"

"Witnesses" was written underneath.

His mobile rung. It was Marshall, he was in the car park and on his way up to the Incident Room. He was collecting a computer wiz on the way. George turned off his phone, stood up and walked out of his office and along the corridor.

After he turned the corner, he heard the lift doors open behind. He looked round and there was Derek Marshall, walking out with a very overweight man in his thirties, carrying a computer tower.

"Sir." Marshall said. "This is Kevin O'Donnelly, part of the IT department."

"Kevin." George gave him a nod.

The IT man rolled the tower around his belly and offered a hand for George to shake.

"Glad I can be of help." He panted

The three of them walked through the door at the end of the corridor into the conference room. Ron Lamden was in there with the uniformed officers. More piles of statements had appeared on the table from the door to door enquiries. The photograph of Steven Armitage had been moved to a position next to the crime scene photographs. There was also a school picture of Teresa Gore. On seeing it George remembered her from the arrest of Sam Tindall. She looked young for her age, thin straight brown hair and an almost toothless grin.

After some discussion with the constable using the computer, Derek and O'Donnelly were able to get the tower to be plugged in to her monitor and use her keyboard. When Derek gave the nod, George and Ron took positions either side of Kevin's large form. They watched the screen.

"I don't know if you know it, but everything you look at on the internet is stored. Memorised?" Kevin said to the screen.

"So each site that this guy has visited is logged in the hard drive. Now if he's knowledgeable about computers, he might clear the history. But from what Derek has told me, he's an old sod, so he won't know about that. Let's see"

Ron looked to George and they both shrugged their shoulders.

"Here we are. See?" Kevin asked.

He pointed at the screen. There was a white screen with lists of words and abbreviations.

"Oh yeah." George answered. He didn't have a clue

"Now let's open these up" Kevin carried on.

He tapped at the keyboard and the display on the screen changed several times until the whole screen was filled with tiny photographs. It was impossible to tell what they were of, but there was a theme to them. They were all flesh coloured. George leaned in, to get a closer look. As he did, Kevin tapped some more and one of the images filled the screen.

"Jesus Christ!" George shouted and recoiled from the image

It was clearly a child.

"Christ, shut it down or something" He said.

Kevin tapped again and the image shrunk back to the size of a stamp. He closed the file and opened another. It was more of the same. He went to close that one down, when George spoke.

"Hang on. How many photos are there?"

"In that file? Two hundred and thirty items. They all look the same."

"I'm sorry Derek, but I need to know if there are any pictures of Teresa Gore in there. You'll have to check them for me."

"Oh Jesus. Do I have to sir?"

"Sorry mate. It's got to be done."

George stood up straight and looked at his watch. It was gone four. He left Ron with instructions to talk to Johnson again and charge him with possession of the images for now. Then he made his way to the meeting.

George got the lift down to the first floor and walked ahead when the lift doors opened. As he walked along the carpeted corridor, he was thinking about why McClintock had asked to see him in this room.

The Chief Inspector's office was on the third floor. He reached the second door on the left and reached for the handle.

The door opened inwards and was at the far end of the room, so when George opened it, he saw the wall with two blue display stands in front. One had the Hampshire Constabulary Badge and the other had the Crimestoppers logo. He was aware that the Chief Inspector was speaking and as he kept on walking, he saw McClintock sitting at a table.

"No more questions? Ah. Here is the Detective in charge of the investigation, DI George Finney."

As George kept pushing the door, he was aware of people sat facing McClintock, a room full of people and they pointing cameras. As he came in to their view the room filled with the sound of shutters and flashlights. McClintock had his arm stretched as a welcome and had a reptilian smile on his face. George was stunned. Visibly stunned. He saw the chair to the left of the Chief Inspector, sat down and rested his arms on the table.

"So what can you tell us, Inspector Finney?"

George had no idea where the question came from.

"Erm. The investigation is proceeding as well as can be expected. Erm, house to house enquires are taking place and erm, we have had two people helping us with our..."

"With due respect Inspector, we have covered this already with Chief Inspector McClintock. Perhaps you can give us the very latest information."

"Err, um. The..."

"What about the search of the flat in Prospect Lane. Did that yield anything?"

George's jaw dropped. His mouth opened and closed a couple of times, but no sound came out. He couldn't believe he was in this situation. Who had told these people about such recent events.

McClintock took over, "The search took place and a computer was removed from the premises. I will keep you informed with any developments."

George looked at him dumbstruck.

"So is there anything you do want to say Inspector?" The voice again. "Inspector?"

George was silent for a second, until he could finally get himself to speak.

"We are still hoping for anyone who saw Teresa Gore on Thursday evening to let us know. That is what we need at the moment, any sightings."

"Well gentlemen, that will be all for this Press Conference. I will notify you of any new announcements. Otherwise, the next conference will be the same time tomorrow. Thank you." McClintock said.

With that, the journalists, photographers and film crews starting breaking down their equipment and leaving the room.

George turned to McClintock and took his glasses off. He was struggling to contain his anger.

"Don't you ever do that to me again." He said through gritted teeth. "In future, if you want me to perform at a Press Conference, you tell me."

"You were late, George. If you were here on time you would have known."

"And where's the sense in telling them about Prospect Lane? We haven't fully processed the information, you can't just go shouting about it."

McClintock looked across the room to make sure none of the journalists had heard.

"This is nearly the twenty first century, George, and this is the modern way of policing. They are broadcasting twenty-four hours a day, rolling news, instant reaction. We have to take advantage of it, so they can help us."

"Help us?" George replied. "Help you, you mean."

And with that he stormed out of the room. He had to force his way past the journalists who were walking in the corridor. One of them called out to him.

"Anything you can tell us? Off the record!"

George kept on walking and said. "No comment. No bloody comment."

George started the next day in a slightly better mood, but not much. When he had got home on the previous evening, his wife had made light of his TV appearance. She had told him that he had looked like a fish out of water, gasping for air. They didn't play back his comments, just voiced over his image. He accepted her joking but had a troubled night's sleep. It gnarled him how McClintock was using the case. He was worried that the press were being too well informed. He was afraid it was going to bite their bum.

The case also was making him restless. He was satisfied that they had two arrests in the second day. But he wasn't confident that either Armitage or Johnson were the killer. There was no proof of the girl being at Johnson's flat, and none of the photographs were of her. Fiona Wells had come back from searching Emily Gore's house with little of use. George wondered whether Armitage had another place nearby that he used, which would have some evidence. There was the possibility of a motive with him, but something nagged at the back of George's head. It was telling him that there was someone else. He needed a break, a sighting, someone who had seen Teresa Gore before she died. He got that break at eight forty, on Wednesday morning.

The whole team were in the Incident Room when his phone rung. It was from Sergeant Longe at Havant. The door to door enquiries had uncovered a possible sighting by an old lady on Friday morning. George took the details and summoned Ron. They were going visiting.

The biggest delay for them getting to West Leigh was trying to turn right out of the Police car park. Everyone would have given way or left a space for a marked car, but nobody noticed the silver Civic. After forcing his way out, to a chorus of horns, he made good progress and twenty minutes later he was parking outside the flats in Millbrook Drive.

The two of them got out of the car.

"Time for a fag, Guv?" Ron asked.

"Yeah go on, quick one." George replied.

It seemed a bit cooler than of late. It was still warm and sunny, but there was a breeze making the air fresher. While Ron puffed, George looked at the flats. It was a two-storey block, with two doors. Four flats in each part. There were a lot of these in this area. They generally housed old residents, but every so often the council would put a nuisance case in one of the flats. George imagined that the council had a theory that the older people would guide the younger misfit, and all would turn out hunky dory. That was never the case. It always meant misery for the older ones, as they had to put up with excessive noise, disturbances, strange people hanging around and sleepless nights. Looking at this block, it was the same. Three windows with clean pretty net curtains and one with a blanket draped across the glass.

"Ready Ron?" he asked.

"Yep. Thanks Guv."

They walked in and tried the door. It opened, meaning the security lock had been broken. Inside their footsteps echoed around the concrete hallway and they went to the door downstairs, on the left, under the steps. Ron pressed the bell.

A face appeared behind the reinforced glass and the door opened. George was surprised to see that Elsie Norris wasn't as old as he expected. She looked about fifty and was dressed in a blouse and trousers which were covered with a purple tabard. George took his warrant card out of his jacket pocket and held it up.

"Hello. I'm Detective Inspector Finney, this is my colleague Detective Sergeant Lamden. You spoke to one of our officers about Teresa Gore?"

"Oh, that was Elsie. She's in here. Do come through." The lady replied.

The real Elsie Norris did look as old as George expected. She was a large lady sitting in a high-backed armchair, facing the window, in her living room. She was wearing a pink cardigan over a flowery summer dress, and there were pink slippers at the end of her bandaged legs. She looked up at the two detectives.

"Elsie? It's the police about the little girl, Teresa. They're detectives." The lady said from the living room door.

"Ooh, they're big ain't they?" Elsie said and her face broke in to a big toothless smile. With her large glasses, she looked like a happy frog. "Sit down boys, make yourself comfortable."

They took their places on a brown settee, loaded with cushions, against the right-hand wall.

"You like 'em big, don't you Else? Would you two like a cup of tea? I'm just doing one."

Elsie chuckled and the two of them accepted the offer.

"That's Tina." Elsie said. "She's my home help. I can't do as much as I used to. Well, I am eighty-five."

"Eighty-five? Never." Said George.

"Yes. I'm eighty-six in October. If I make it, that is."

"Well you do look good for it, Elsie. Can I call you Elsie?"

"Of course you can love." Elsie said, shuffling to face them in her chair.

"Well, my name's George and this is my colleague, Ron. You saw one of our policemen yesterday evening. He was asking people whether they had seen Teresa Gore."

"That's right. He came round about five o'clock. When he knocked, I thought it was about upstairs. You know." She nodded towards the ceiling.

"They're always in some sort of bother. They say hello and that, but I try not to get involved."

"That's probably the best way, Elsie. You told our man that you had seen Teresa. Is that right?"

"Yes. I did it was…"

She stopped as Tina had arrived with a tray, laden with cups, saucers and a teapot. George was surprised by seeing it. Whenever he made tea at home it was always a bag in a cup. There was no space on the coffee table, so Ron leaned forward and moved some of the magazines. George scanned around the room while this was going on. It was clear Elsie was a grandmother. There were photographs of younger adults and then children. He turned to his right and looked out of the window. Through the nets he could see the bush moving in the breeze, but not much more. When he turned back, the tea had been poured and Tina had disappeared from the room.

"You were saying Elsie?"

"Oh yes, sorry. When you get to my age you forget these things. Yes. It was on Friday. I remember that for sure, because it was the twelfth and that was my wedding anniversary. It would have been sixty-three years if Daniel was still around. Sixty-three years, it was hot then as well." Elsie was staring in to space. Watching her memories being played back.

"Daniel was a lovely man. We never argued, you know. Never a cross word. He was so patient, you see. He'd been a prisoner of war in Burma and seen some horrible things, but he never took it out on me. And I used to know if he was remembering stuff and I'd just leave him for a bit, then put my arm around him. Thirteen years now. Since he's gone."

Ron looked to George, who shook his head. He was happy to let Elsie tell her story in her own time. He noticed her eyes were watery. He drunk some of his tea and gently tapped his cup with the saucer. The slight noise brought Elsie back and she continued.

"It was Friday morning. I'm always up early in the mornings. Twenty odd years working the early shift at Kenwoods has meant that I'm always up at five. And everyday, I get my paper from Gibbons, around the corner. Tina says that I should let her bring it in. But I want to try and get out while I can, and it is only just around the corner. You know, on the corner of Forestside."

George nodded.

"And I'm always his first customer. I'm there at six o'clock everyday, just as he unlocks the door. And that's what I did on Friday. I went around there, got my paper and come out. And that's when I saw her."

"You know of Teresa Gore, do you?" George asked. Ron was writing notes.

"Oh yes. Everyone around here knows about Emily Gore and her kids. They're trouble ain't they. My friend, Joyce. We go to the club together. It's every Thursday and a bus picks us up and takes us to St Clare's over in The Warren. She lives in the flats next door to them. Poor love, the stuff she has to put up with. So I knew it was her, the girl."

"And where was she?" He was leaning in.

"The milkman was talking to her halfway up Oakshott Drive. Well, if I'm honest, it looked like he was telling her off."

Elsie recognised George's puzzled look.

"Well, I could tell he was pointing his finger at her. Sort of jabbing. Like that" She was doing the action.

"And I know that she's stole milk from him in the past. It's probably been the mother sending her out to nick it."

George leant back against the cushions and raised his eyebrows to Ron.

"Elsie?" Ron asked. "Do you know who this milkman is?"

"Of course I do, love. It's Tony. He's my milkman."

It was Ron's turn to lean back as he blew a quiet whistle. The two detectives sat for a moment in silence, allowing the news to sink in.

"There was something funny. Later on." Elsie said. Both them leaned forward again.

"Go on" George said.

"Well. On Fridays, he collects his money. He comes back in the afternoon, just after one. Last Friday, when he came in, he was wearing his jacket."

"Right" George said, not understanding what she had meant.

"Well it was hot wasn't it. Very hot. Over ninety degrees, they said. But he was wearing his jacket, see? And he was sweltering, you could see he was boiling. And when I saw him in the morning he was wearing a yellow T-shirt. It's part of their uniform, you know. So I said to him, I said, 'What are you doing wearing that great big jacket?' and he said, 'Oh, I have to keep it on, 'cause I had a bit of a problem earlier.' That's what he said."

George was thinking and nodded his head gently. He looked to Ron and tipped his head slightly to the window, to indicate that they were done. He cleared his throat and was about to speak.

"Oh my." Elsie said. She was staring blankly at the coffee table. "No. It must have been nothing."

George looked at Ron and back to her. "What's up, Elsie?"

She turned to them. "It must be nothing. I don't won't to say something to get anyone in trouble."

"You won't get anyone in to trouble, my love. What is it?"

"Thinking back. He came in to collect his money. Now Tina sorts out my change and that, and puts it on the table there ready for him to collect. He sat down, where you are now, talked for bit. I asked him about his jacket and that. Then he took his money and left some change. Now thinking back, I'm sure he had blood on his hands."

Her hand came up to her mouth with look of concern on her face.

The two of them put their teacups on the table and were up and standing straight away. George leaned down and put his hand gently on Elsie's arm.

"Thank you, Elsie. You've been a great help. Thank you."

They made their way out of the flat, Tina followed them to the door and shut it behind them. Outside they stood by the car, before getting in. Ron took out his cigarette packet and started lighting up.

"We'd better have a word with this milkman hadn't we. Sharpish." George said and got in the car. He started the engine and gave it a rev or two. Ron looked at his cigarette. He had only taken one drag, so begrudgingly threw it onto the road.

The drive to the dairy depot didn't take long. At the end of Millbrook Drive, they turned left in to Wakefords Way. The blue Police tape was still in place, and while there wasn't as much activity, there were still a couple of uniformed officers keeping guard. At the end of Wakefords, they crossed over to Middle Park Way, which they followed until turning left in to Dunsbury Way. The dairy was on the left, next to a Funeral Directors.

Whilst driving, George asked Ron to phone and arrange for a SOCO team to come to the dairy to examine the milkman's float and an officer to watch over it. They parked on a car park outside the single storey building, got out of the car and walked to the entrance.

They walked past two large gates into the depot. A wide concrete drive led down to an open yard. The building was on the left, with a four-foot-high dock running its length. They climbed the steps up to the office door, which was open. There were a few milkmen walking along the dock and going from one door to another and out again. George looked in the office for a manager or supervisor. An older milkman called out from behind him.

"Can I help chief?"

George turned and saw a short man in his early sixties. He had thick glasses, long greying hair and a grubby uniform.

"Yes, we're looking for a boss."

"Oh, he's down the store. At the end there."

They walked along the dock to a dark doorway at the end. As they passed the open doors of the fridges, cold air and the smell of sour milk hit them. When they walked in to the store, they saw a stout man, wearing a shirt and tie, behind a counter serving a milkman. He walked off to different areas of the large room and returned with an armful of cartons of fruit juice. He saw George and Ron and, straightaway, knew they were CID.

"Yes chaps, how can I help?" He said.

"Are you the manager?" Ron asked.

"Yes. Paul Lucas. How can I help?"

"Police. We need to have a word." Ron looked at the milkman. "In private."

"Ah, okay. Matt, get Doug to check you off."

He walked around the counter and they followed him back along the dock. He led them into the office.

Two rooms had been knocked in to one. The first was well lit and had a counter, window and cash office on the left-hand side. On the right-hand side, there was a coffee vending machine at one end of a work surface and a strange object at the other. A milkman turned from the counter and plugged a device in to the contraption. The second room was dark, with a table in the middle and plastic chairs around it. There was a door on the far left-hand side. Lucas took some keys from his pocket and unlocked the door. He opened it and walked through. On the other side was a window lit, carpeted office. There was a desk, Lucas sat down in a leather chair behind it and signalled for them to sit on the two chairs on their side. They stood.

"You've got a milkman called Tony? Delivers in Oakshott Drive." George said.

"Ur, yes. Tony Gibson."

"Is he back yet?"

"Tony? He's round 268. No, not yet. He'll be back in about twenty minutes."

"Right. We need to know when he gets back."

Lucas nodded.

"Do you have a list of his customers?"

"Yes. Luckily, he's on the Roundsmaster, so we can give you full details of his round."

"Roundsmaster?" George was puzzled.

"It's a handheld computer. Replaces books. In the old days, all the roundsmen had rounds books, and we didn't have a clue about their customers. But we've started giving them a computer. Which makes their life easier and after they plug in, gives us all the information about their customers. So I can do a printout which will tell you who they are and what they've had."

"Will it tell us who had a delivery on Friday?"

"Yes. No problem. Shall I print one off?"

"Please."

Lucas got up and led them back out to the front office, locking his office door behind them. He took them to the corner, to the side of the door, near the cash office. There were two windows in this corner, one looking out at the dock, the other the gate. Both had bars on them. Ron looked out of the gate window.

"What's this Tony look like?" He said.

Lucas had sat down in a chair in front of a keyboard and monitor and started typing. He looked out the dock window. Some milk floats were alongside the dock.

"It's hard to say, really."

He stood and looked out the gate window towards the road.

"There he is, coming down the road, in the three-wheeler."

George gave a nod to Ron and they both made their way out of the office. Two milk floats with crates of empties on the back were parked beside the dock and another had parked alongside them. The three milkmen were taking crates of returned milk from the vehicles to the dock. The old milkman was checking them off. At the bottom of the steps, George saw the three-wheeled float stop behind a waiting Transit van to form a queue.

Both doors were folded back on Tony Gibson's float, so Ron went to the far side, George the nearside. Gibson was looking at his handheld computer. As they got closer they heard a chugging noise, a printout was spooling out of the unit. Gibson looked up and was startled by the sight of the two detectives.

"Tony Gibson?" George said.

"Yes?"

"I'm Detective Inspector Finney, this is Detective Sergeant Lamden. We're investigating the murder of Teresa Gore. I wonder if we can ask you some questions."

"Um, okay. Yeah."

"Are you happy to come down the station?"

"Oh, okay. Shall I drive down later on?"

"Well, what I'd like you to do is park your float up there, out of the way. And then we can drive you down there. Is that okay?"

There wasn't a choice. He agreed. George and Ron stepped away from the float, Gibson pressed the foot pedal and the float whined forward.

"Stay with him, Ron. I'll get that list from in there." George said and then made his way back to the office.

Ron trotted to catch up with the Gibson. He drove the float to the end of the drive, where there was a large concreted yard. It was the size of a football pitch, running from left to right. The left side went behind the depot building and had a pair of locked gates at the end. The right side went behind the Funeral Director's and had a lorry's trailer stood in the centre. Its sides were open and the two milk floats that had unloaded were parked alongside. One milkman was on the trailer stacking the crates being passed up by the other. They stopped and watched Ron walking behind Gibson's float. Open fronted sheds lined the full length of the yard, with parked floats recharging in their bays. Gibson drove straight from the drive, across the yard and stopped behind a blue Ford Sierra estate that was parked in a charging bay.

"Alright if I move my car out and put my float on charge?" He called out.

"No, leave it there. Won't be long and we'll be dropping you back." Ron lied.

Gibson went to gather up his stuff from the cab.

"Don't worry about that. Like I said, we won't be long." Ron said. He wanted SOCO to see everything.

Gibson stepped out of the float and walked back towards the drive and the entrance gates. Ron moved beside him, ready to grab if he needed to. The sunlight was reflecting on the concrete making it difficult to keep their eyes open. The milkman on the trailer had crouched down, so he could talk to his colleague. They kept watching.

As they got near the gates, George came out of the office and down the steps. He had a bundle of paper in his hand. The three of them walked out of the entrance and Ron indicated where their car was. A dark blue Fiesta drove up and stopped in the car park. It was the pool car from Fratton nick. It didn't need to be marked to scream out 'Police Car'. George gave his keys to Ron and walked over. There was a man and a woman sat in the Fiesta, he didn't know their names, but had seen them around.

"Alright?" He said through the opened passenger window. "It's the milk float straight in front of you. Behind a Sierra. See if there're any traces of blood and anything that will connect him to the girl. Okay?"

They both nodded. The man said. "We might need to take it back to Fratton, to have a proper look."

"Yeah, whatever. I trust you'll do a good job."

He moved from them and was about to walk to his car when he saw the marked car arrive. It drove towards the entrance and stopped on the left of the drive. A Constable got out and straightened himself up and put his helmet on. George recognised him as the young PC he had seen on Monday morning.

"Hello young man. Stafford. Isn't it?" He said.

"Yes sir."

George could see the young policeman's chest swell because his name had been remembered. It was handy that he had written it down on Monday.

"Your job is very simple, Stafford. You make sure that nobody gets into this depot that shouldn't do. Okay? Especially press. Understand?"

"Yes sir. I'll do that." More posturing from the Constable.

"Good man. Have fun!"

George walked back to his car and got in. Ron was sitting in the passenger seat, Gibson sat behind him. Both were silent. George looked through the car windows at the policeman, who looked like he was muttering to himself, like he was rehearsing some lines.

"Bless him" he said and then started the engine and drove off the car park.

PC Stafford stood upright and proud at the entrance to the dairy, every so often he would walk from one side of the drive to the other. He was happy. He'd been in the Police force for eleven months and he had enjoyed most of it.

He had grown up in Wilmcote House, in Somers Town, Portsmouth. A good kid in a notorious block of flats, in a bad area. This meant he was a victim of bullying for most of his life. The way most people survived in this area, was to turn a blind eye, to keep your head down and just keep yourself to yourself. But Ben Stafford couldn't do that. If he saw something wrong, he couldn't allow it to go unpunished. Not that he was going to do the punishing. He was a frail skinny lad, who couldn't punch his way out of a paper bag. So, he would go and report the wrongdoers. He couldn't count how many times he had been beaten up between the ages of seven and seventeen. What started off as petty kids' fights, developed in to nasty assaults. But he didn't learn, he still couldn't let it go and would tell the police who it was that attacked him. He was lucky to survive the last beating. He had been knocked to the ground and kicked in the head by Eddie Tyrrell and his three brothers. He was unconscious for two days. The Somers Town beat officer visited him in his hospital bed. He said that Ben had three choices... Move away. Stay, and be killed. Or stay and fight back by becoming a copper.

When Ben came out of hospital his lifestyle changed completely. He joined Bob Muller's Gym in Southsea, took up boxing and pumped himself up. Within six months, he was a different person. His first application to join the police was declined, because he was too young. Instead he worked as a bouncer for a night club in Southsea and three years later he was successful.

He enjoyed his work, especially when he was part of the team that arrested Eddie Tyrrell for burglary. His face was a picture. Stafford even enjoyed days like this week, where he had spent all day standing guard. Monday at the roadblock, yesterday and the first part of today at crime scene. He knew he was doing an important job. He had even managed to be seen on TV. The news crews had filmed him standing by the blue tape, next to the copse. His parents had rung him to say how proud they were. And today, it was his responsibility to keep the press out of the depot. He was in charge.

After he had let a couple of milk floats in, he saw a silver Volkswagen van park next to the kerb on the road. Three men got out and walked towards the entrance, one had a camera. He was going to be on telly again. One of the men was wearing a light grey suit, with a shirt and tie. His face was familiar. Stafford had seen him on news reports but didn't know his name. The three approached the Constable and stopped in front of him. The cameraman lifted his video camera to his shoulder and started filming past the policeman down the drive. He could clearly see the Forensics team working on Gibson's float. The second man had sound equipment strapped over his shoulder and the reporter looked Stafford in the eye and gave a friendly smile.

"Hi. Chief Inspector McClintock told me that you would be here." He said.

"Yes?"

"It's because of the arrest of the milkman, isn't it."

"Yes, that right."

"So he was arrested?"

"Yeah. Two detectives just took him away."

"And the Forensics? I guess they're looking for blood and traces of evidence linking him to the murder of Teresa. Is that right?"

"Oh yes. That's why I'm here, to make sure no one can contaminate the crime scene."

"So the crime occurred in the milk float?"

"Certainly looks that way." Stafford was pleased with himself. He had given the impression that he had some knowledge about the crime. He wanted the reporter to know that he was important.

"They've got him. That's for sure." He added. He'd heard about sound bites. Powerful little phrases that summed up a situation. They were bound to use that one.

"Is it okay if I have a chat with the dairy manager?" The reporter asked.

Stafford shook his head and smiled.

"No. I've got my instructions. You have to stay this side."

The last words were drowned by the sound of a large lorry and its horn. An articulated lorry with a trailer displaying the logo for Sunshine Dairies had driven off the road to go into the depot. Stafford, the cameraman and the soundman moved to the right of the entrance to get out of its way. The reporter moved to the left. The lorry moved forward into the entrance and stopped before the length of the trailer was in. This created a screen for the reporter, who quickly run up the steps and walked into the office.

Lucas was about to walk out to deal with the delivery when the reporter appeared in the doorway.

"You the manager?"

"Yes, can I help?"

"Yeah, Chief Inspector McClintock has sent me. He's asked if you can get me the address of the arrested milkman." The reporter said. It was a gamble, but worth trying.

"Oh. Well I've got the delivery, um. Here are I'll get it for you."

Lucas went into the cash office and ducked down behind the counter. The reporter was silently urging him to be quick. He nodded at a milkman who walked in. The manager reappeared with a small box file. He opened it and starting flicking through the cards. The reporter looked out through the door, the lorry's brakes gave a hiss and it began to lurch forward slowly. When he turned back, Lucas was walking out of the cash office with a piece of cardboard in his hand.

"Here you are. You might as well keep it. Shouldn't think we'll be seeing him again."

The reporter took the card and quickly walked out of the office and back down the steps, stuffing the card in to his jacket pocket. When the lorry's trailer cleared the entrance, he was back in his original position. He tipped his head towards the van and the other two followed him back to the Volkswagen. They had twenty minutes to prepare for the next live bulletin.

George parked his Civic in the car park of Kingston Crescent Police Station and all three men got out of the car. They walked through the rear entrance and straight to Interview Room 2. Ron opened the door and extended his arm as a welcome for Tony Gibson.

"Make yourself comfortable." He said, indicating the chair on the far side of the table. "Would you like a coffee or something?"

"Er, a coffee would be great, thank you."

"I'll bring it in a few minutes, okay? So sit tight." Ron said, then closed and quietly locked the door.

The two detectives made their way to the Incident Room.

When they walked in, Fiona Wells and Derek Marshall were sitting in their usual places at the table.

"I've got some news." George said. "Good news, I hope."

He put the bundle of paper on the table, walked to the map and made sure he had their attention.

"We now have a sighting of Teresa Gore. She was seen by a lady called Elsie Norris at six o'clock on Friday morning, in Oakshott Drive." He pointed to the location.

"She was seen with the milkman in the area, who we now know is Tony Gibson. It is said that he was having a go at her. It is also reported that later in that day, he appeared to have blood on his hands. It may be correct to say that Teresa Gore was alive at six o'clock and dead before one." George leant forward to pick up the bundle.

"We have Tony Gibson downstairs. Fiona, I would like you to see if he has any history. Derek, this is a complete list of his customers and their deliveries. I would like you to co-ordinate the questioning of every customer on this list. We need to know if they also saw blood or noticed anything unusual. Okay?"

"Yes sir."

"My Nan had a milkman." It was Fiona. She seemed to be talking to herself.

"She used to say that you could set your watch by him."

"Pardon?" George asked.

"My Nan. She used to say that her milkman delivered the same time, every day, whatever the weather. It was more likely that her clock would go wrong, than him being late."

Derek pulled a face. "So?"

"I was just saying."

"I think you've stumbled across something, Fi." George said. "Derek, also ask those customers if he was late."

"Right. Yeah, I get it. Sorry Fi." Derek said.

"Me and Ron are going to go down to question him. So off you go, go get busy."

He passed the bundle across the table and left the room with Ron following. They picked up three coffees from the canteen on the way down. Had they had more time or if they were interested, they would have seen the silent television in the far corner. If they had seen the television, they would not have liked what they saw.

The reporter was standing in front of the dairy speaking to the camera. At the bottom of the screen it announced 'Breaking News' and the scrolling headlines read 'Milkman arrested in connection with the murder of eight-year-old Teresa Gore. The suspect named as Tony Gibson was arrested by two detectives today. Forensic teams examine milk float, which is considered to be the crime scene.' The image changed from the reporter to footage of a Scenes of Crime Officer examining the cab of the milk float, then cut to a close up of PC Stafford mouthing, "They've got him. That's for sure."

Tony Gibson looked up when the two detectives walked into the Interview Room. Ron put a coffee cup on the table in front of him.

"Thank you." He said.

"No problem. Here's some sugars if you have them." Ron said and dropped a couple sachets next to the cup. Gibson picked up one, shook it, ripped the top and poured the contents in to his coffee. George sat down opposite and looked him over.

Gibson was a slim, strong looking man. He was well tanned from working outdoors and had short cropped blond hair. He was wearing a blue polo top with a Sunshine Dairies logo embroidered on the chest, and blue trousers. He looked presentable. George imagined that customers like Elsie Norris would consider him as 'a nice young man'. His heavily bitten nails might have been an indicator that he wasn't a confident person. At the moment, he looked very nervous.

"So, Tony." George said, after having a sip of coffee. "I'd like to point out that you are not under arrest. Okay? We merely need to ask you some questions and it is better all round to answer them here, instead of at the depot. Alright?"

Gibson nodded.

"DS Lamden here will take notes. Okay? Good. So let's start at the beginning, shall we? Is Tony Gibson your full name?"

"No, it's Anthony, with an aitch, Ian Gibson." He leaned forward to see that Ron was writing the correct spelling.

"And, how old are you Tony?"

"Thirty-one."

"Married?"

"Yes. With two kids. Two girls, six and four. They're funny names, but they'll get used to them." Gibson sniggered at his own joke and then stopped himself when he got no response.

"And how long have you been a milkman?"

"Oh, um, eight years, just. I've always been on round 268, West Leigh."

"So that's quite a while isn't it. You must be part of the community."

An electronic tune starting playing the Nokia ring tone. All three went for their pockets. It was Gibson's phone. He looked at the display.

"It's my wife, sorry. I'll ring her back later." He rejected the call. "I'll turn it off. Sorry, where were we?"

"Part of the community?" George said with a sigh.

"Yeah, I suppose I am really. I look out for the older customers, make sure they're okay and that. I've stumbled across some burglaries as well, in my time."

"Really? And did you report them?"

"Oh yes. I rang 999 on my mobile. The police came out straight away and caught them."

"Well done. That's very good."

"Just part of the job, really."

"Hmm." George looked at Gibson for a second or two.

"So you're familiar with the Gore family."

"Everyone knows Emily Gore. She bumped me once, so I don't deliver to her any more."

"Bumped you?"

"Yeah. Done me for some money. Not a lot, because I was careful, see? When I took over the round, I was warned about her. She had only been in the house a few months and she'd already ripped off the other dairy that was going at the time. So I didn't serve her. Then after a while, she comes out and catches me. Says she's got welfare vouchers and could I deliver. So I started, but she had to give me them in advance."

"Welfare vouchers?"

"Yeah, they get them from the Social. It entitles them to seven pints of milk, free. We accept them and pay them in and then get the money back later. On my round, I get loads of them."

"Right."

"So all's going well and then one day, she don't give me her voucher. So I thinks she's alright now and keep delivering. Stupidly, I did it for about four weeks and she'd never answer the door, or send the kids out and say she's not in. So I stopped, but she had done me for about twelve quid."

"Okay Tony. Thank you. Perhaps, we can bring it up to date then. Can you tell me anything about Friday, just gone?"

Gibson sat thinking and then shook his head slightly.

"Trouble is, with this job all the days merge in to one. You do the same thing every day, you can't tell one day from another. Friday? I guess it would be just the same as every Friday."

"It was very hot last Friday. If that helps."

"Umm. No. Still can't think of anything special."

"Well. Let's put it this way, Tony." George said, slightly more firmly. "We've been told that you were seen talking to Teresa Gore on Friday."

"Oh God, yes! That was last Friday" Gibson hit his head with his hand. "Yes, sorry. Like I say the days just merge in..."

"Yes, you did say that Tony. So what about last Friday?" George had an edge to his voice.

"Erm, well, I've been having a lot of milk stolen recently. You know, off of the doorsteps. And I've seen the Gore girl walking about. She seems to be wandering around really early. Given her age, she should have been tucked up in bed, but I wouldn't be surprised if her mum has been sending her out to nick stuff. Well, on Friday I saw her walking from Forestside into Oakshott. I thought that I'd caught her out, because I hadn't delivered there yet. She was walking up the road as I was delivering down it. So when we were level, I stopped the float and crossed over to talk to her. To be honest, I let rip at her. You see, it's been frustrating having so much stuff taken. One day I had a whole road cleared out, everything taken. And because I'm franchised, it comes out of my own money, the depot don't reimburse me. So I warned her, threatened her, in an effort to stop her taking my stuff."

"And what time did you see her?" George asked.

"I'm in Oakshott Drive at six o'clock on Fridays. So it would have been just after then."

"So you didn't think to tell the police that you had seen her?"

"Why?"

"Why?" George barked. "Don't you read the papers? Don't you watch the telly?"

"No."

"You're supposed to be a part of the community and you didn't know that an eight-year-old girl had gone missing."

"No. Honest." Gibson's voice was getting higher. "I only deliver there, I don't live there. None of my customers said anything and I don't read the paper or watch the news. The first I knew of anything going on was on Monday, when Wakefords Way was closed off. And I saw the coppers standing by the woods yesterday and today."

"So you're telling me that you knew nothing about Teresa Gore going missing."

"Yes. No. I mean I didn't know!"

"Well. You were the last person to see her alive." George said.

The colour drained from Gibson's face. George stared silently at the milkman. He waited for a minute before speaking.

"Is there anything else about Friday that you remember now?"

"What do you mean?"

"Someone told us that you may have had blood on you."

Gibson sat looking at his hands and then looked up at the detectives.

"I remember now, I had a nosebleed on Friday. I always get them, get them all the time. It's my blood vessels, they're very weak so the slightest thing starts them off. I try to make sure I've got tissues, but on Friday I didn't have any. It just happened to be a day when I had a really bad one. It just gushed out, all over my shirt. I didn't have any way of cleaning up, so I put my jacket on. Kept it on for the rest of the day."

"A nosebleed?" George looked at Ron and back to Gibson. "You had a nosebleed."

"Yes. I did."

More silence. George was thinking that something about Gibson didn't make sense. It was as if he was telling the truth. Ron put his pen down and lent back in his chair. George went to take his glasses off when suddenly Gibson stood up, his chair falling backwards. He started screaming.

"Oh my god, oh my god, oh my god! I've just realised where this is going. You think it's me! I was the last to see her, I had blood on my clothes. You think it was her blood, you think I killed her! I didn't touch her, I shouted at her, that's all. I didn't do it. I'm not a killer." He was standing with his hands on his head.

"Jesus Christ! Shit, shit, shit, shit. I've just realised something. The policemen. They were standing by the woods, near the lay-by, in Wakefords Way. Is that where they found her? Is it? Is it? I went there. I go there all the time, I use that path. I have a piss there every week. Jesus Christ I might have pissed on her. Holy shit! I don't ..." His words were lost in the start of a panic attack.

Panting heavily, he leaned on the table struggling for breath. George stood up slowly, while Ron got up and put Gibson's chair back in place.

"Sit down Tony." George said quietly.

Gibson sat. His face was red, his eyes watering. Slowly his breathing calmed down. Ron returned to his chair.

"Tell us about the woods, Tony. In your own time." George asked.

Gibson's red eyes moved from George to Ron.

"On Fridays and Saturdays, because I'm on the round longer, I need to take a leak. There aren't any loos on the round, so I go into the woods just by the lay-by. I go in by the same place where the policemen were standing. I walk in a short distance and have a pee in the bushes, on the right-hand side. If that's where she was, I might have pissed on her."

George sighed deeply, he put his glasses back on and looked at Gibson. He spoke slowly and surely.

"Tony, let me make this clear. We are investigating the murder of Teresa Gore. An eight-year-old girl. We are going to do everything we can to find her killer. You are not under arrest, you are helping us with our enquiries." He paused to let it sink in.

"However, to be honest, in answering our questions, you have put yourself in the frame. You have made yourself a suspect. The last reported sighting of Teresa Gore was with you. By your own admission, you had a go at her, and on Friday, were covered in blood. And you've just told us that you used the pathway in the woods, putting you near a crime scene. Now we want to find the killer. If what you are telling us is true, we need to substantiate your story and eliminate you from our investigation. Then we can move on to find the real person. Does that make sense?"

Gibson nodded.

"We need to get the clothes you were wearing on Friday. Will you allow us to do that?"

"If it helps clear me, yes. But they have been washed though."

"That's fine, we have people who can deal with that. So you're happy for me to send someone to pick up those clothes and anything else we need to help you. If DS Lamden writes up something, you'll be happy to sign it?"

Gibson nodded and George looked to Ron, who started writing an authorisation request. George knew he was chancing it, he wasn't playing by the book, but he wasn't breaking any rules. He knew as soon as they arrested Gibson, a clock would start ticking. They would have limited time to get enough information to charge him. Also, solicitors would be involved and they generally stalled any investigation. By doing as much as he could now, with Gibson's consent, he would save time later. The milkman signed the piece of paper and unwittingly gave consent for the police to take anything they wanted.

He gave his address, described the items of clothing and said that his wife would be home. The detectives were about to leave him in the room with a promise of more coffee, when George remembered something.

"Oh yes. Tony, I'll be sending someone down to get a sample of your DNA. They'll take a swab of your mouth, that's all. It's something new and it will help clear you." He said and then to himself. "Or convict you."

In the Incident Room George heard from Fiona that Gibson had no criminal record, not even a parking ticket. He wasn't surprised. He sent Fiona out visit Gibson's home with someone from Forensics. As she left he felt satisfied with their progress. They seemed to be getting somewhere. All was going well. He had no idea how wrong he was.

The first news report may have made a few waves, but the second caused massive fallout. In a longer piece the reporter again named Tony Gibson as the man arrested in connection with the murder of Teresa Gore. The footage of the Forensics team examining the milk float linked with film of the Gore house and the copse where she was found. Also in this broadcast, the names of the two other men who had been arrested were included and film of Johnson's flat in Prospect Lane was shown. A close-up shot of the Gosport House sign and the door to his flat, left no doubt as to where he lived.

The BBC reporter had drawn the other broadcasters to follow his route, both Sky and ITN were broadcasting live and national and local radio had picked up the story. Their reports included interviews with other milkmen outside the depot and residents in the round 268 area.

On seeing these broadcasts, some of Gibson's customers telephoned the depot and cancelled their deliveries. Lucas, the depot manager, was at a loss to explain why he was getting all kinds of abuse from people. The phone was red hot with cursing and threatening callers. Why did they think that he had employed a child killer? He'd only been at the depot for a year.

Gibson's mother-in-law watched the news report open mouthed. She telephoned her daughter, Laura, while it was still on air.

"Tony's on the telly." She said

"On the telly? Don't be silly. What would Tony be doing on the telly?" Laura replied.

"They're saying he killed a girl. An eight-year-old."

"What? What are you saying?"

"It's on the telly, love. Now. They're saying that an eight-year-old girl that lived on his round was found murdered, and that he did it. He's been arrested."

"There must be some mistake." Laura was crying now. "I'm sorry mum but you must have got it wrong. Get off the phone I'm going to give him a ring."

"I'm coming down." But there was no one on the other end.

Laura put the phone down on her mum and picked up to dial her husband's mobile. It rang for a few rings and then went to voicemail. She didn't leave a message but cut off and redialled. This time it was straight to voicemail. He had switched his phone off. She went over to her television and hesitantly switched the power on. She didn't have cable or satellite, so flicked through the four channels. Nothing about Tony, perhaps her mum was wrong. She switched on the hi-fi system and tuned in to Power FM. Still no news. She sat on the edge of her settee, waiting.

In West Leigh, a crowd of residents had gathered on the green outside Gosport House. They were made up of young mums and delinquent youths looking for any excuse to start trouble. They were shouting and screaming abuse at an empty flat. Johnson's partner had decided to stay with a friend after the search. A pair of youths ran into the block and up the stairs. When they got to the flat, they took spray paint cans from their jacket pockets and sprayed across the windows and door. One had written 'PEDOS OUT' in black over the reinforced glass. This brought cheers from the crowd below. As the day progressed, this crowd got larger and larger and they decided to move to the homes of other suspected paedophiles in the area. Uniformed officers from Havant had to come out and contain the crowd. This was another opportunity for the lowlifes in the group to start fighting. All of this began to be played out in front of camera crews, who on hearing of the violence arrived from the dairy.

None of this would have caused George too much bother, but the arrival of a solicitor in Robert Johnson's police cell was going to drop a huge fly in the ointment.

Charles Holmes-Wood would be considered by everyone who met him as a pompous little man. He didn't care. He knew that all people had a place in life and his was above all the others. His florid complexion and shock of yellow blonde hair made him stand out in a crowd, as did his fondness for striped jackets, which never closed across his large stomach. He had known Johnson for a while. They shared the same interests, but he preferred to keep his fondness for children as a holiday exploit, visiting Thailand and Vietnam regularly. It was he that managed to keep Johnson out of prison after the school incidents, and he managed to reduce the number of rape charges to just one. Defending

Johnson was a huge responsibility for him. He had to do it, and do it well, because Johnson had the potential of derailing Holmes-Wood's life.

The discovery of child pornography on Johnson's computer set alarm bells ringing for the solicitor. He had forwarded some of the images. There was a very real chance that he was going to get roped in to this. It was in his best interests to halt the investigation, not just get Johnson off the hook, but force the police to stop where they were. He had listened to the reports from West Leigh on Radio 4 in his car as he was driving down from Winchester. By the time his Mercedes C220 had merged from the M3 on to the M27, he had a plan. When he arrived at Kingston Crescent and walked into the cell, he said four words.

"Leave it with me."

He walked out of the building, off the police station's grounds to the pavement and started dialling on his mobile phone. Half an hour later, he had enough cameras in front of him to begin.

"Gentlemen." He said, ignoring the women in the huddle.

"Thank you for coming at such short notice. I have always trusted the English legal system. I always believe that justice will come through. The foundation of such belief is the fact, that in our law, we approach cases with the mentality of 'Innocent until proven guilty'. We have a court system which allows jurors to decide the fate of a defendant. Even for the most trivial of cases, a magistrate decides whether a man is guilty or not."

He paused while looking for the best suited camera to speak to. The one he chose had a reflection of the police station on its lens. It was going to make the perfect shot.

"However, Hampshire Constabulary has seen fit to sweep aside all these foundations in law. Using the media, it has decided to accuse people in such a way, that there is no chance of a fair hearing. The public has been told that three men are guilty of some of the most hideous of crimes. Hampshire Constabulary has allowed the men's details to be broadcast. This will have tarnished the view of any prospective juror or magistrate. Should they wish to continue in this manner, I am issuing a warning that they will face a legal challenge which will take in to account the defamation of the three men's characters. Thank you, gentlemen. That will be all."

A flurry of questions were thrown at him but he ignored them all, posing for still photographs to be taken with the police station in the background.

The BBC reporter wasn't at Kingston Crescent or West Leigh. He knew that at some point the story would move to Tony Gibson's home. Having taken the address card from the depot, he told his crew that would be their next destination. After his last broadcast, the team got back in the Volkswagen and he directed them to the A3(M). From there they drove south, joined the A27 and left at the Eastern Road. This took them into Portsmouth. They turned left at Milton Road, right at Priory Crescent then right again in to Carisbrooke Road. They drove slowly looking for Ruskin Road. To their right, the houses backed onto Fratton Park. They found it, second road on the left and turned in and stopped on the left-hand side. Gibson's house was halfway along the road. The reporter expected a wait before they would start filming, so he told the other two to sit tight and got out of the van. He walked along the road towards the house. It was in the middle of the terrace, with a bay window, small forecourt and low front wall. It looked presentable and fairly well maintained. He walked past, on to the end of the road, crossed over and walked back to the van. Got in and made himself comfortable.

After fifty minutes, a dark blue Ford Fiesta drove into the road from the far end. It was closely followed by a marked police car. The cameraman got out of the van and crossed to the right of the road. He moved to a position behind a parked car and was able to get a view of the front door of Gibson's house. The two cars parked, a female detective and a man with a silver case got out of the Fiesta, while two uniformed officers got out of the marked car. In his viewfinder, he could see them walk to the door and ring the bell. A dark-haired woman opened the door. By zooming in he could tell she had been crying and there was a look of horror on her face when she saw the police. She let them in. The reporter had come alongside him. He explained what he had shot and then they waited. Twenty minutes later the door opened. He lifted the camera up and started shooting. All four officers were carrying something. There was a computer tower, a clear bag with clothing, another with video cassettes and a bundle of evidence bags. The dark-haired woman stood at the doorway, staring at them as they got into their cars. She looked to her left and saw a woman in her fifties hurrying along the pavement. She run to the woman and hugged her. The two of them were crying as they walked back into the house. The footage was exactly what the reporter wanted and would be perfect for the next report.

There had been some changes in the Incident Room. The plastic cover over the map on the left-hand wall had been wiped clean and redrawn. The roads which made up round 268 had been highlighted in red and the locations of Gibson's meeting with the girl, the Gore house and shallow grave written in black. The flipchart had the following written on it... LAST SIGHTING 6.00AM, BLOOD ON CLOTHING – GIRLS? BLOOD IN MILK FLOAT – GIRLS? MORE SIGHTINGS? WOODS?

George and Ron were in discussion at the corner of the table.

"He's a bit unstable, Guv." Ron said. "With that reaction."

"Hmm. Perhaps he's going over the top to try and convince us he's innocent. Just need some results back from the Forensics to nail him."

They looked up when the door opened, expecting to see DC Wells or Marshall. They were both surprised to see McClintock.

"Ah, George." The Chief Inspector said. "Can I have a word?"

He looked at Ron and added, "Outside." Then left the room.

George pulled a face at Ron and got up from the table. He walked out into the corridor to see McClintock disappearing around the corner. When he got there, he saw him standing outside Finney's office. As he walked closer, he could see the Chief was sweating heavily. He leaned across to open his door and allowed McClintock to walk in. They took a seat either side of the desk.

McClintock rubbed his face with the palm of his hand before speaking. George thought that he looked tired, which made him feel a little happy.

"Er, Gibson." The Chief said. "You arrested him?"

"No. We've been having a chat. You know, he's been helping us with our enquiries. And he's been very helpful, since he's put himself in the ..."

"You've got to let him go."

"What?"

"Gibson. You've got to let him go. Now."

"Let him go? Why? He's looking like a prime suspect. He was seen with the girl, he had blood on his hands. He's our man."

"You have to let him go now, George. He can't stay locked up. Do you understand? His solicitor is downstairs..."

"Solicitor?" George interrupted. "He hasn't got a solicitor. Why has he got a solicitor? Who called him in?"

"His solicitor brought himself in. His name is Charles Holmes-Wood."

"Holmes-Wood! What's that obnoxious little shit doing here? That's a sign of guilt for sure, if he's your solicitor."

"He's just held an impromptu press conference outside the station. He's accused us of sentencing three men by the media. Their names have been broadcast and we're prejudicing a jury. Johnson's flat has been attacked by a mob and now they're roaming the streets looking for anyone who looks like a paedophile. We have to let them all go."

"What do you mean sentencing by the media?"

"Our constable at the dairy told a reporter that we got him, Teresa Gore's killer."

"Reporter at the dairy? Who told them? I only rung you up to ask for SOCO and a bobby, I didn't..." It suddenly dawned on George. He took his glasses off, put them on the table, shook his head in disbelief and then looked at McClintock in disgust.

"It was you wasn't it. You told the press and now it's all blown up in your face. Well you've really fucked up. Sir." He stood up and walked to the window.

"George, there's a scheduled press conference organised for four o'clock, again. I'd like you to present our side of the story, put us in a better light with the public. But in the meantime, we have to let the three men go."

George turned from the window and stood with his hands in his pocket.

"Let them go?" He shouted. "Are you kidding? One of them has confessed to having sex with an eight-year-old, one has over two hundred and fifty pornographic pictures of kids on his computer and the last one was seen with blood on his hands after being seen with a murder victim. And you say we have to let them go!"

McClintock squirmed in his chair. He struggled to look at George because the light behind him.

"Look George." He looked down at his hands. "I need your help. Okay? I've admitted it. I've screwed up. Big time. I know you'll be able to handle the press conference. That will get us back on track, but we've got to get those three out of this station. Today. Look, if we put Johnson and Armitage out on police bail, we can keep a track on them and we can get them back in later. But the milkman, we have to leave him alone."

George went to react, but McClintock held his hand up.

"Holmes-Wood will skin us alive if we go near him. You need to let him go and check him out from a distance. You can't touch him unless we have something concrete. I mean it George, concrete."

George couldn't take anymore. He picked his glasses up from the table and walked out of his office without saying a word.

"You'll be there at four George, won't you? George?" McClintock said to a closing door.

Thursday 18th July 1996

George was there at four. All the photographs in the national papers proved it. Black and white images of him, stony faced, sat beside an uncomfortable Chief Inspector.

McClintock's hope that all would go back on track was wrong. His suggestion to release the three men quietly while the press conference was running, didn't take in to account the conniving mind of Holmes-Wood. The solicitor had made his own arrangements to keep the story bubbling and keep the pressure on the police. All the tabloid papers carried Tony Gibson's story, with The Sun having the exclusive interview. Its headline screamed "Set up – I was framed by Hampshire Police." There was a large photograph of Gibson looking downtrodden, with Holmes-Wood looking smug in the background.

Needless to say, the mood in the Incident Room was very grim. The CID team were sitting at the left-hand end of the table with piles of documents and statements in front of them. George broke the silence.

"Ron. What's the latest about the milk float?"

Ron sighed, thumbed through some sheets until he found what he was looking for.

"Well Guv." He said. "They brought it back here to go over it thoroughly. Got it picked up on a low loader and now it's in the shed, out the back. Um, there's plenty of blood in the cab. Spots and splatter all over the place. But none of it's the girl's. They've gone over the whole float, in the boxes, under the bed where the batteries are and there's nothing. No trace of Teresa Gore on that float."

Ron threw the paper back on the pile. George rubbed his bald head, his elbow resting on the table. He looked to DC Wells.

"Fiona?" he said.

"We were lucky to have visited Gibson's house when we did. Once Holmes-Wood got his hands on him, we wouldn't have got any evidence. We were able to take the clothes he'd been wearing, which had been washed, so the Forensics guy also took the filter from the washing machine. We took another jacket, just in case. We took some videos cassettes and his computer, as well. The cassettes and computer had porn on them. Hard stuff, but not kiddies. There were still blood stains on his polo top, but they weren't Teresa's group. SOCO's working on the filter and going over the clothes closely, but so far there's nothing relating to her. No hair, no fibres, nothing."

She finished and saw George's face and added, "Sorry."

"Derek?" George asked.

"We've been calling on his customers, sir. There's been a fifty-fifty split amongst them. Half have said they can't believe he would do such a thing and the other half are ready to lynch him." He leant across to pick up a bundle of statements.

"There is general agreement that he was wearing his jacket when he started calling for money. That's about seven o'clock, well from five to, one of the customers said. There were comments about him having blood on his hands, which might have come from them listening to the press. But one did say that when Gibson opened his jacket to get his wallet, she saw a large stain on the left of his chest. He's got some customers on Wakefords Way, opposite the entrance to the copse?"

"Yeah, I know the ones." George said.

"Well, there's a woman there who has seen him go in the woods and come out again. In her words he must have been having a comfort break. Always seemed to be when he was calling back, about elevenish, on Fridays and Saturdays."

Derek stopped. The three detectives sat looking at George, who now had his head in both hands. He puffed loudly and his hands moved in to a praying position and he rested his chin on his thumbs. He stared directly ahead.

Half a minute passed, then he opened his hands and clapped them together.

"So it's all a coincidence then." He said. "The day that Gibson is seen having a go at the girl, just happens to be the day she disappears. He just happens to walk round with blood on his clothes and hands on the same day that she's murdered. And if it's his DNA on her, it's because she just happened to buried at the place he has a piss. It's all a bloody coincidence!"

Fiona felt brave enough to speak.

"Timing is the issue Boss." She said.

"Hmm. Derek, did any customer say he was late at all?"

"No sir. Not one. He was usual time throughout the day." Derek replied.

146

"Guv?" It was Ron. "Do you think you're wanting it to be him? So you're seeing it that way."

"Eh? Come off it Ron, what's the chances of all these things happening on the same day?"

"Well" Ron took a breath before continuing. "The chances aren't as high as you might think."

He waited, but George didn't explode, so he continued.

"Look, if Teresa Gore wandered the streets as much as she did. Gibson might have seen her every week. Look at the map, look at his route, their paths were bound to cross. So it was no big thing that he did see her on that day."

"Alright Ron." George said. "But why didn't he report it? Eh? It was in the local rag on Saturday and Monday. Why didn't he tell us? And what about the blood?"

"It was in the local rag Guv. I don't read it, so he might not. And like he said, he doesn't live on the round, so he's only seen his customers on Friday and Saturday, which was before it went in the paper. With the blood, if he really does have nose bleeds as often as he says, he might have blood on his hands every week. Customers have only thought about it since they've heard the news reports."

Derek was nodding his head in agreement. George felt as if he was the only one who could see sense.

"Tell me this Ron." He said. "Do you reckon you wouldn't see a kid buried in the ground, if you were having a piss. Do you? He was there on Friday and Saturday, and so was she!"

"I'm sorry Guv, but you've got to try and look at it differently. I hate to say it, but you're being blinkered. Like Fiona said, you've got to look at the timings. What you're saying is that he killed the girl just after six o'clock, took her body half a mile up the road, buried her, got rid of every trace of her from his milk float, delivered milk to over fifty customers and was still on time to collect his money at ten to seven!"

"Well, how did he do it then?" George shouted.

"Guv, He might not have done it." Ron was almost pleading.

"Argh!" George slammed his hands on the table. "Well you fucking well find who did it then! I'm going out!"

He stood up and stormed out of the room, walked down the corridor and thumped the lift call button. The lift took him to the ground floor, where he walked straight out through to the car park. He decided he needed to walk, so followed the building round to Kingston Crescent, then headed towards Mile End Road. It was clear he was angry, anyone who stepped in front of him was going to regret it.

It was about half an hour before he started to think. It was as if he had woken up from a daze. He walked past The Theatre Royal in Guildhall Walk and realised that he had no recollection of passing hundreds of shoppers while going through Commercial Road. He was heading south. As he walked across a pedestrian crossing, he began to consider what had happened.

It had been a long time since he had lost his rag like that. He always had a temper when he was younger. He'd learnt to control it, but there were times when he was on the beat in Portsea that he lost it. That was part of the reason why he'd earned so much respect from the toughest families in the area. They had a motto... Don't Fuck with Finney. But he hadn't exploded like that with his team for a couple of years. That was probably the first time DC Marshall had experienced it. But what caused him to flip this time? What was it that made him so wound up, so frustrated?

Were the others right? Was he getting blinkered about Gibson? Had he lost his knack or was he getting past it?

Was it the girl? Teresa Gore had been the youngest murder victim he had to investigate. He'd experienced dealing with youngsters who had been killed in accidents. There was the case of the two kids in the fire, which was sickening to deal with. But each time a youngster died, he considered it a terrible waste. In this case the girl had suffered such a bad life, her brutal end might have been thought of as a release. But to spend just eight years on this planet and then die in such a savage way seemed so... so wrong. Was it this that touched a nerve?

Or was it Gibson? There was something about the milkman that didn't fit as far as George was concerned. He looked like a decent bloke, he was a family man, married with two young kids. But something jarred. It was the coincidence thing. George didn't believe that so much could be a coincidence. And there was the way he reacted in the Interview Room. He was too naive, too ignorant, too innocent! If it hadn't been for McClintock, he would have pushed Gibson more and more until he broke.

McClintock. Perhaps he was the reason? For years George had tolerated the Prima Donna ways of his superior. His vanity and ambition were something to take the mick out of, but they had never affected an investigation. This time, the Chief Inspector's desire for publicity had destroyed the case. This was the reason why George felt the way he did. He felt he had the killer in his grasp, and now he wasn't allowed anywhere near him.

His aimless walk south had taken him through St Paul's Road, across Kings Road, down Great Southsea Street and in to Castle Road. He decided he would walk along to Marmion Road, before dropping back into Snookies on Osborne Road for a coffee.

In Marmion Road, he was passing a charity shop when something caught his eye. In the window, on a display stand was a small white plate, about four inches wide, with blue decoration, a piece of Delft. The shop's door was wedged open, so he went in.

It was bright inside the PDSA shop. The walls had been painted white and it looked clean, but there was a lingering smell of second hand clothes. The carpeted floor sagged as he walked around the fixtures to the shelves at the far end of the shop. He scanned them to see if there were any other items of pottery. There was nothing of interest to him, except the sign showing the CCTV symbol with the warning 'Shoplifters will be prosecuted'. He sighed as he read it, thinking it was a sign of bad times that people would steal from a charity shop. He made is way to the glass counter which had two elderly ladies behind it. One was sitting, reading a newspaper. The other, who was standing, smiled at George as he approached.

"Hello." He said. "You've got a plate in the window, on the right-hand side. How much is it? Please."

The woman looked to where he was pointing, and then looked down at the other woman.

"That plate, Maureen. Is it three pounds?" She said.

Maureen looked up.

"In the window? Yes, three pounds, Joyce."

Joyce looked at George.

"It's three pounds. Sir."

George found himself smiling at the daftness of the situation.

"I'd like to buy it please. If that's okay?" He said.

"Righto." Joyce said and made her way round the counter and over to the window.

Maureen went back to her paper and then looked back at George. She did a double take.

"Is that you?" She said, holding The Sun's front page up and pointing to the smaller picture.

153

George visibly sagged. "Yes."

"Look at that Joyce." Maureen said. "We've got someone famous in our shop."

Joyce was walking back with the plate. She looked at Maureen, whose fingers hadn't moved from the photo, and then at George, who was smiling in a forced manner.

"Oh yeah. Well that makes both of them then."

"Yes, that's true, Joyce. We've got the full set."

George did not have a clue what they were on about, and it showed.

"Sorry love." Joyce said. "But what with you coming in here, that makes both of you. Him, he's a regular."

It was her turn to point at the paper, this time at the photo of Gibson.

"Yes, he comes in all the time." Maureen said. "Buys LP's and stuff. Probably won't see him now, he'll get a big payout from this story."

Twenty minutes later George was standing on the pavement, outside the shop, with a carrier bag of shopping in his hand. He had phoned DS Lamden and asked to be picked up. He also spoke to the Forensics team to see if they had taken the milk float back to the dairy depot. When he heard they hadn't, he gave them his instructions. A car horn sounded. Across the road, Ron had stopped in his Green Rover.

"Thanks Ron." George said as he got in.

Ron knew there would be no apologies. Nothing would be said about what had happened. That was the way it was. If Finney blew up, he blew up and then that would be it. Over. Forgotten about.

"Where to Guv?" He said.

"Ruskin Road, Ron. Please."

"Guv. You know you can't go near Gibson."

"It's alright Ron. I know what I'm doing."

Ron slipped the Rover in to drive and pulled off. He drove to the end of Marmion Road and then straight over the crossroads. His route was through the back streets of Southsea. It was less distance, but there was plenty of stopping and giving way in the narrow roads. Eventually he reached the end of Haslemere

Road and went over Goldsmith Avenue to enter Ruskin Road. He stopped in a space on the left-hand side. He looked over to George, who was pulling something out of the bag. It was the plate.

"Ron, look at this. If I told you that this plate was a hundred and thirty years old and could be worth over two hundred quid, would you believe me?"

Ron thought for a moment, he could handle the explosions but not lectures about plates.

"I dunno." He said.

"Ron, would you believe me?" George asked again.

Ron shrugged. "Yeah. I suppose, why wouldn't I?"

"Exactly. Why wouldn't you." George answered. He stared at Gibson's house, nodding.

"Right, now drive to the dairy, please. Okay Ron?"

"Alright Guv. You sure you know what you're doing? I don't want you to get in trouble."

"Don't worry Ron, just drive."

As Ron moved off, George removed a notepad and pen from his jacket pocket. They made their way to Priory Crescent and then turned left at Milton Road.

When they turned right to go towards the Eastern Road, George made a note on his pad. He did the same, when they reached the roundabout to join the A27. The last note he took was as they were turning left in to Dunsbury Way.

There were no TV crews near the depot now and they parked on the car park outside the building. George asked Ron to wait, while he got out of the car and walked towards the entrance. He looked down the drive and then towards the road. A handful of milk floats drove into the depot as he waited. And then he saw what he was waiting for, the police low loader with the Gibson's milk float on it. The driver drove towards the entrance and was flagged down by George. After a brief exchange, he was back in Ron's car with a smile on his face.

"Right Ron, back to base." He said.

Friday 19th July 1996

Tony Gibson was struggling to deal with the events of the previous 48 hours.

This time on Wednesday, he was going about his usual business. The same daily routine... same place, same time, everyday. And then his life was turned upside down.

Now he was in the luxury of The Post House Hotel, Southampton. Charles Holmes-Wood had negotiated this with The Sun for his story. His family were moved to this near penthouse suite for their own safety. So, while he was enjoying expensive food and a stylish apartment, it was a sweetener for an uncertain future.

He had phoned his boss at the depot and been told not to return. It wasn't that he wasn't innocent, Paul Lucas had said. It was just that the round had been decimated by the publicity. And there would be no guarantee to Gibson's wellbeing while he was walking the streets of West Leigh.

The hotel was no place for two young kids. The six-year-old kept asking awkward questions, while the four-year-old was having tantrums for her missing toys. There was only enough time to grab a bagful of clothes."

Laura, his wife, said that she believed he was innocent. She said that. But it felt to Gibson that she didn't really mean it. He could sense her mistrust, there was a feeling of doubt. He was sure she had kept herself awake until she knew he was sleeping and woken up before he did. She had spent hours on the phone talking and crying to her mother. Even as she sat watching the television now, it seems she had one eye on him.

Holmes-Wood said that all of these things will be taken in to account when the compensation is sorted. He had told him that his old life no longer existed. He couldn't turn the clock back. His life had changed and someone was going to pay for it.

The door buzzer rang. Perhaps it was someone from the paper. He opened the door.

"Anthony Ian Gibson. You are under arrest on suspicion of murdering Teresa Gore on Friday 12th July 1996. You do not have to say anything. But it may harm your defence if you do not mention when questioned something which you later rely on in court. Anything you do say may be given in evidence."

The two detectives were standing side by side. George stepped forward with handcuffs and locked one bracelet on the hand Gibson was holding the door with. The milkman stared at it frozen in disbelief. His wife looked from the television and started screaming, the two girls responded by crying. The noise was terrible. George grabbed the other hand, cuffed it and held on to the chain.

"We're going for a drive Tony." He said.

"I'll need my solicitor. I want him there." Gibson said. He was starting to cry.

"Oh don't worry, he'll be there. We've told him already." George said and led him away.

Tony Gibson was back in Interview Room 2 with his solicitor sitting beside him. They stopped talking when the door opened and George and Ron walked in. George was carrying a sealed tape cassette. He sat down opposite Gibson and began to unwrap it.

"Well gentlemen, I think I should advise you that the video cameras in the two corners of the room are working, so everything is being filmed." He said.

"You're making a grave mistake Finney." It was Holmes-Wood.

"It's Inspector Finney to you. Charles." George hissed.

He had written on the label of the cassette and put it in to the built-in tape recorder on the table. He pressed the play and record buttons.

"I've advised my client to say nothing." Holmes-Wood leant back in his chair, his hands behind his head.

"That's good." George said. "Because we're not talking to your former client. Go for it Ron."

"Charles Holmes-Wood. You are under arrest for electronically sending images containing pornographic images of children. You..." Ron continued with the caution.

The solicitor at first looked confused and then threw himself forward and stood with his hands on the table. His red face had turned scarlet.

"This is preposterous! You wait 'til I've finished with you. You'll be lucky if you're giving out parking tickets." Spittle flew out as he spoke.

"Finished?" George said calmly.

There was silence. Holmes-Wood took his seat, he was breathing deeply as if preparing for the next round.

"Computers, Charles? Do you know much about computers?" George asked, but he wasn't waiting for an answer.

"You see, I don't know much about them. But we've got a lad upstairs who's a bit of a wiz with them. You could say he's big in computers. And he says that everything that is sent by e-mail has a sort of stamp on it. I think he calls it an IP address. And this address says exactly who sent the items. So, say for instance, you sent a picture of yourself doing something to a five-year-old Thai boy. He would be able to say that it was your computer that sent it. He can then even look at the details of the photo and say when it was taken and what camera was used. It's all clever stuff. Really." He smiled smugly.

Holmes-Wood gripped the table, his knuckles were white. He was thinking how he was going to word his statement.

"You won't be able to prove a thing. I regularly let other people use my computer. There will be no proof that I have sent anything. Only that it came from my computer." He said.

George laughed. Gibson looked at Holmes-Wood.

"The problem you've got Charles is that your fat arse has so many moles on it, it's kind of... unique."

The solicitor was dumbstruck. Ron stood up and took his arm and pulled him to a standing position. George stopped the tape, stood up and looked at him.

"We're going to put you in a cell for now and one of our colleagues, who deals with maggots like you, will talk to you later."

He turned to Gibson.

"There's a duty solicitor waiting in reception for you. Unless you've got a decent one."

Gibson mumbled something.

"What?"

"I said, I haven't got one." Gibson answered.

"We'll send him down."

Half an hour later, they were back in their same seats. The duty solicitor sat quietly next to the milkman. George had put a new cassette in to the recorder and started recording. There was a folder on the table in front of the detectives. George sat in silence for a few seconds, looking over Gibson. He reached in to his right-side jacket pocket and pulled out the small plate.

"See this plate Tony." He said. "If I told you that it was over a hundred years old and worth hundreds of pounds, would you believe me?"

Gibson looked puzzled. He had no idea what the plate had to do with anything.

"I suppose so, why wouldn't I?"

"Hmm, there's that 'why wouldn't I', Ron. You said the same didn't you."

Ron nodded.

"Yeah, why wouldn't I. Hmm."

George paused and put the plate on the table.

"Oh, by the way. Tony, you are under arrest now and you are being recorded. You know that, don't you? You understand, don't you?"

Tony nodded.

"Sorry Tony, but the tape doesn't pick up nodding."

"Yes." Gibson said. "I understand."

"Good." George rubbed his beard. "When we talked the other day. There were a lot of coincidences, weren't there? Involving you and Teresa Gore. Now, I'm not big on coincidences myself. I don't tend to think that many things like that happen by chance, you know. But it's funny. See this plate. I saw it in a shop window. I just happened to be passing and there it was. It was in the PDSA shop in Marmion Road."

He watched Gibson's eyes. There was a flicker.

"And it just happened to be a shop that you regularly visit. I mean, what's the chances of that. In all those different shops in Southsea, I happen to see a little something I like. And it turns out to be the same shop that you use. What are the chances, eh? What a .... No, I won't say it."

Gibson gulped. In the quiet room, it sounded very loud. George continued.

"You mentioned that your job put you in the same place at the same time every day."

Gibson nodded and then said. "Yes."

"Must be annoying I suppose, having no variety in your work, quite mundane. Or I suppose it could be a good thing, you do know exactly where you are going to be at a particular time on any day. I guess you drive to work the same time also. Regular as clockwork, I guess. Which way do you go? Eastern Road? Must be the shortest, quickest route, isn't it?"

Gibson just nodded. George let it pass.

"Yeah, we went that way yesterday. Didn't we Ron? Drove to the depot and that. Oh yes, I nearly forgot. We did you a favour as well. Got your car picked up. Well it was stuck there in the bay. You weren't able to get there after being whisked off to Southampton, were you. It's in a shed out the back."

George could see Gibson was starting to sweat. His skin began to take on a waxy complexion. There was a chance that he was going to be sick. He waited a full minute for he carried on.

"We didn't go back to see Elsie. You know, Elsie Norris? The lady in the flats in Millbrook Drive? No, it wouldn't have been fair, would it. I mean, she thought she was helping us with our investigation. Instead she playing a part in your cover story, wasn't

168

she? You see, I had a look at the distance between the paper shop and the alleyway in Oakshott Drive and it's about seventy to eighty yards away. I don't think Elsie, with her eyes, would've been able to see you clearly talking to anyone. But if you told her that you had had a ruck with the girl, why wouldn't she believe you."

Gibson was staring at the table top, he didn't see the solicitor glance at him and shift his chair slightly away.

"I'm now going to show Tony Gibson some photographs." George said for the recorder.

Ron took out a small handful of 10 by 8's, which were face down. He slid them to George. George turned them, so he could see the fronts.

"CCTV Tony. Closed circuit television. Funny isn't it. You go about your daily life and all the time you're being watched. These are stills from the camera at the end of the Eastern Road. You know, on the roundabout, where it joins the A27. And they prove something Tony. They prove that you're right in saying that you are in the same place at the same time every day. Look."

He laid them down. There were nine black and white photographs showing the north and south lanes of the road. Two lanes either side of a concrete divide. In the outside lane of the northbound side was a Sierra estate, indicating to turn right at the roundabout. On the bottom left hand corner of the photo was a display of the date and time.

"You see these prove that you are at this junction everyday around two fifty-two in the morning. See? Friday 5th, Saturday 6th, Monday, Tuesday, Wednesday, Thursday, Friday and Saturday. Everyday, same time."

George looked up at Gibson. He noticed a slight smirk. It was only very slight, but it was there. Smugness. George looked back at the photos and acted as if he had just noticed something.

"Um, don't know what's happened here though."

He pushed one of the photos forward so that it was in front of Gibson.

"Something different with this one. Friday 12th July. It says that you were there at twelve twenty-eight. That would be nearly two and a half hours early."

Gibson eyes widened. He kept his head down, looking at the photo. George indicated to Ron, who removed two more photos from the folder.

"Did you know that the charity shop had a camera in it, as well? Probably not, I should imagine. I mean, surely nobody steals from a charity shop. But they do, so that means the shop has to film what goes on."

He turned the two colour pictures so they were the right way round. He pointed to the first.

"This is you, isn't it? On Thursday afternoon. Buying some clothes. The ladies said they were some of the worst clothes the shop had. They'd been on the rails for months and then you went and bought them. A ghastly hooded anorak and some hideous trousers. That's how they described them. Apparently, you told them that you were buying them for a fancy dress party. I think they said you called it a 'bad taste' party. Hmm, bad taste."

He pointed to the other picture.

"And this is you on Monday afternoon. Bringing them back. All washed."

George sat back and folded his arms across his chest. He stared at the top of Gibson's head, who was still staring at the table.

"You got a dog?" George asked.

Gibson looked up, his eyes were red.

"You see one of the things about having a dog is this. You can wash your clothes. You can put them on the hottest wash, you spin them as fast as possible. But when you take them out of the machine, there'll always be a dog hair attached. You just can't get rid of them. And it's not just dog hair, Tony."

Gibson closed his eyes and hung his head.

"And as for cars, Tony, there are so many different places that are difficult to clean. Thoroughly."

George waited.

"I know you did it Tony."

Gibson lifted his head. His mouth was tightly closed. He looked in to George's eyes. It was as if he was planning what to say. A minute passed. When he spoke, his voice was dry.

"No comment."

And that was how it stayed. Three hours of questioning. No comment.

It was at times like this that George wished it was like the movies, where they confessed all and said why they committed the crimes. But they never said why.

The Crown Prosecution Service was happy that there was enough evidence to support George's theory. He believed that Gibson had left early on Friday 12th, wearing the charity shop's clothes over his own, so he could either pick up Teresa Gore or any random person walking around at that time of night. Traces of blood and hair proved that the girl had been in his car. It was likely that she was killed there. Despite a wide search, they never found the murder weapon. After he buried her in the copse, he changed from the blood-stained clothes, drove to work and then carried on as normal.

George reckoned that Gibson set out to use his daily timetable as his alibi. Then by putting himself in the frame, he knew that it would appear that there was no time for him to have attacked the girl. Especially as he had fed false information to Elsie Norris.

George kept thinking about how lucky he was to have seen the little Delft plate in the window of that shop. If he hadn't stormed out of the Incident Room, he wouldn't have been there. How lucky was he! What were the chances! What a coincidence!

He lay down on his bed and looked at the underside of the top bunk. The lights had been out for a while now in his cell, where he was waiting for his trial. He heard snoring from above. He started to think about what he had done. He had been wrong.

It was meant to be the perfect crime.

The planning had gone on for years. It all started when he found the chisel in a customer's garden. He picked it up, put it in the box in his milk float and starting thinking.

He had chosen the right victim. Nobody cared about the Gore girl.

He'd tested whether Laura would wake up when he got out of bed early, two months before. She was such a deep sleeper, she had no idea.

That morning, he saw her walking in Nursling Crescent. He stopped the car beside her. The silly cow thought he was going to talk to her. He got out and straight away put a bin bag over her. She was so small and it was so big that it covered her from her head to her knees. He wrapped his arms around her legs and scooped her up. He opened the car's tailgate and threw her in. With one foot on her, he started to wrap her in gaffer tape so she was bound. Then he drove to the northern half of Prospect Lane, where it's rural and deserted. He stopped in a lay-by and moved her to the front seat. Back in the driving seat, he shouted at her to stop crying. And then he started. The chisel was in his left hand, point downwards. He swung his arm across her chest over and over until his arm ached. She was quiet.

He was proud of how he had got rid of the chisel and the bloody bags. When he got to work, he put them in his float's rubbish box and threw the lot in the depot's rubbish bin. He knew that the bin men were going to empty it at nine o'clock that day. By the time the body was discovered, it had been buried in a landfill site miles away. He should have thrown the clothes in there too. If he had, he wouldn't be where he was now. Instead he had washed them in the launderette on the corner of Lawrence Road and then taken them back to the shop. A perfect plan if it hadn't been for Finney. Lucky bastard.

He smiled at the thought of going into the copse and pissing on her body Friday and Saturday.

But he failed. It wasn't the perfect crime.

His wrist started to throb and his warm blood was seeping through his clothes. Stupid wardens couldn't see that they didn't have all the pieces from the broken plate.

He might have failed before, but he wouldn't fail now. No one was going to find him until they unlocked the cell at six o'clock.

And by then, he would be gone.

Printed in Great Britain
by Amazon